The Widow's Christmas Courage

MIRIAM BEILER

Contents

Chapter 1

Sarah's hands tightened on the reins as the familiar outline of Maple Creek came into view. The late November wind nipped at her cheeks, carrying with it the bittersweet scent of fallen leaves and wood smoke. She took a deep breath, steadying herself for what lay ahead.

"*Mamm*, look!" Emma's excited voice piped up from beside her. "I can see the *schoolhaus*!"

Sarah smiled despite her churning stomach. "*Jah*, that's right, Emma. We're almost there."

As they clip-clopped down the main street, Sarah's eyes darted from building to building, noting the changes - and the things that had stayed the same - in the two years since she'd left. The general store had a fresh coat of paint, and old Mr. Yoder's harness shop boasted a new sign.

But Yoder's Furniture still displayed the same rocking chair in the window. Mrs. Beiler was sweeping her porch just like she always had, if a little more wrinkled and gray.

"Oh, *Mamm*!" Emma gasped. "Is that where you used to work?"

Sarah's gaze followed her daughter's pointing finger to a modest wooden building with large front windows. The faded sign above the door read "King's Sweet Blessings."

Her heart clenched at the sight of the darkened windows and the "Closed" sign hanging crookedly in the door.

"*Jah*, that's it," Sarah said softly. "That's where I grew up."

As they pulled up in front of the bakery, the front door flew open. Sarah's parents rushed out, their faces a mixture of relief and worry.

"Sarah! Emma!" her mother called, hurrying down the steps as fast as her recovering body would allow.

Sarah helped Emma down from the buggy before embracing her parents. "*Mamm, Daed*," she murmured, fighting back tears. "It's so *gut* to see you."

"We're so glad you're here," her father said, his voice gruff with emotion. He pulled back, studying her face. "You look tired, *meine dochder*."

Sarah mustered a smile. "It's been a long journey, but we're here now. That's what matters."

As they ushered Sarah and Emma inside, Sarah's keen eyes noticed a layer of dust covering everything. The usually gleaming display cases were dull, and the air held a stale quality that spoke of disuse.

"I'm sorry it's not in better shape," her mother fretted, following Sarah's gaze. "We've been meaning to clean, but with my illness..."

"Don't worry about it, *Mamm*," Sarah assured her. "We'll get everything back in order."

Her father cleared his throat. "Sarah, about the bakery... We need to talk."

Sarah's stomach dropped, but she nodded. "Of course. Emma, why don't you go explore the rest of the bakery? Just be careful not to touch anything sharp in the kitchen."

As Emma scampered off, Sarah's parents led her to the small office in the back. Her father settled heavily into the chair behind the desk, while her mother perched on the edge of a worn armchair.

"We didn't want to worry you with all the details in our letters," her father began, "but the situation is... well, it's not *gut*."

Sarah's mother reached out, clasping Sarah's hand. "We've fallen behind on our bills, Sarah. The medical expenses, plus having to close the bakery... We're in danger of losing everything."

Sarah felt as if the floor had dropped out from beneath her. She'd known things were bad, but this... "How much?" she asked, her voice barely above a whisper.

Her father named a figure that made Sarah's head spin. It was more than she'd ever imagined, more than she could hope to earn with months of hard work.

"We've been praying for guidance," her mother said softly. "And then you wrote, saying you wanted to *kumm* home... We thought perhaps this was *Gott's* answer."

Sarah swallowed hard, fighting back the panic rising in her chest. "Of course," she said, forcing confidence into her voice. "We'll figure this out together. I have some savings, and with hard work, we can get the bakery running again."

Her parents exchanged a look that Sarah couldn't quite decipher. "There's something else," her father said slowly. "Jacob Zook's bakery... it's been doing very well. He's even talking about expanding."

Sarah's breath caught in her throat. Jacob Zook. She hadn't allowed herself to think about him in years. Not since...

She shook her head, pushing away the memories. "What does that have to do with us?"

"He's offered to buy our bakery," her mother explained gently. "He says he'd keep us on to work here, but... it wouldn't be ours anymore."

For a moment, Sarah couldn't speak. The thought of losing her family's legacy, of working for Jacob Zook of all people... It was almost too much to bear.

"*Nee*," she said finally, her voice firm. "We're not selling. This bakery has been in our *familye* for generations. I won't let it go without a fight."

Her parents looked relieved, but Sarah saw the worry still lingering in their eyes. "We were hoping you'd say that," her father said. "But, Sarah, it won't be easy. The competition is fierce, and our equipment is outdated..."

"I know," Sarah interrupted. "But I have ideas. New recipes, ways to modernize without losing our traditions. We can do this."

Just then, Emma's voice called from the kitchen. "*Mamm*! *Kumm* look at what I found!"

Sarah excused herself, grateful for the interruption. She found Emma standing on tiptoe, peering into an old glass-fronted cabinet.

"Look, *Mamm*," Emma said excitedly. "Are these yours?"

Sarah's breath caught as she saw what Emma was pointing at. A collection of delicate sugar sculptures, crafted years ago, still stood proudly on the shelves. Memories flooded back of late nights spent perfecting her technique and the joy of creating something beautiful and unique.

"*Jah*, Emma," she said softly. "I made those a long time ago."

"They're so pretty!" Emma exclaimed. "Can you teach me how to make them?"

Sarah smiled, running her fingers over the intricate sugar flowers. "Of course, *Liebling*. Maybe we can make some for the bakery when we reopen."

As Emma chattered excitedly about everything she wanted to learn, a spark of hope ignited in Sarah's chest. This was why she'd come home; not just to save the bakery, but to build a future for her daughter and to carry on the legacy her parents had built.

Later that evening, after Emma had been tucked into bed in Sarah's old room, Sarah found herself alone in the quiet bakery. She ran her hand along the cool surface of the marble countertop, remembering all the hours she'd spent here as a girl, learning at her mother's side.

The bakery was always more than just a business to her family. It was the heart of their community, a place where people came together to share in life's joys and sorrows.

The thought of losing it, of seeing it become just another outpost of Jacob Zook's, made her heart ache.

Sarah moved to the window, gazing out at the darkened street. Across the way, she could see lights still burning in Zook's Bakery.

For a moment, she allowed herself to wonder about Jacob. Was he there now, working late into the night? Did he ever think about their past, about what might have been?

She shook her head, banishing the thoughts. It didn't matter. Jacob Zook was her competitor now, nothing more. She had to focus on saving her family's bakery, and on providing for Emma and her parents.

But as Sarah made her way upstairs to her childhood bedroom, doubt sneaked into her heart. The figure her father mentioned loomed large in her mind.

How could she possibly earn enough to pay off their debts and keep the bakery afloat? Her savings would barely make a dent, and with winter approaching, business would slow.

Sarah paused outside Emma's door, listening to her daughter's soft breathing. She'd promised Emma a better life, a chance to grow up surrounded by family and tradition.

But what if she couldn't deliver on that promise? What if, despite her best efforts, she failed? The bakery couldn't be reopened until next week at the earliest.

The weight of responsibility settled heavily on Sarah's shoulders as she slipped into her own room. She knelt beside her bed, clasping her hands in prayer.

"*Mein Gott*," she whispered, "please guide me. Show me the way to save our bakery, to provide for my *familye*. I can't do this alone. Grant me Your wisdom and guidance. Please..."

Sarah climbed into bed, fearing that the challenges ahead, far greater than she'd anticipated, were more than she could handle alone. The bakery needed more than just hard work and determination. What was needed was a miracle.

Sarah's last thought before drifting off to sleep was a desperate plea: How could she possibly support her family and save the bakery with so many odds stacked against her?

Chapter 2

J acob Zook kneaded the dough for his famous cinnamon rolls, his hands moving automatically. The familiar rhythm soothed him, even as his mind raced with thoughts of the day ahead. The bakery hummed with pre-dawn activity, the scent of fresh bread and warm sugar filling the air.

"*Daed*, look!" Samuel's excited voice piped up beside him. "I rolled out the dough all by myself!"

Jacob glanced down at his son's work, a smile tugging at his lips despite his preoccupied thoughts. "*Gut* job, Samuel. You're becoming quite the baker."

The boy beamed with pride, his small hands already reaching for the cinnamon-sugar mixture. Jacob watched him for a moment with a little melancholy. How quickly he was growing!

At eight years old, Samuel was already showing a keen interest in the family business, eager to learn every aspect of baking. Which was just as well since Jacob could use every bit of help possible.

His small storefront was not sufficient for the growing levels of business, even with the employees he'd hired and trained. That was why he'd put in the offer for the Kings' larger storefront. The fact that, if they accepted, he'd have at least two possible skilled employees immediately available was also a tempting bonus.

A little while later, the bell above the door chimed, drawing Jacob's attention. Mrs. Yoder bustled in, her arms laden with baskets of fresh eggs from her farm. Right on time, as usual.

"*Guder Mariye*, Jacob," she called cheerfully. "I've brought your usual order, plus a few extra. I hear you might be needing them, what with the competition heating up."

Jacob's hands stilled on the dough. "Competition?" he asked, trying to keep his voice neutral.

Mrs. Yoder nodded, her eyes twinkling with the excitement of sharing news. "Ach, jah! Didn't you hear? Sarah King Lapp's *kumm* back to town, for *gut*. Word is, she's reopening her family's bakery."

The words hit Jacob like a punch to the gut. He'd known Sarah was back, of course; Maple Creek was too small for her return the previous week to go unnoticed. But he hadn't expected her to reopen the bakery so soon.

Or at all, if he was being honest with himself. Well, so much for moving storefronts.

"Is that so?" he managed, forcing his hands back into motion. "Well, I'm sure there's room enough for both of us in Maple Creek."

Mrs. Yoder clucked sympathetically. "*Ach*, I'm sure there is. But you know how folks love Sarah's pastries. And with her being a widowed mother and all, and with her parents' troubles to boot... well... people will want to support her."

Jacob nodded, not trusting himself to speak. He busied himself with arranging the eggs, his mind whirling. Sarah King.

Nee.

Now it was Sarah Lapp, as she'd been for years.

He hadn't allowed himself to think about her in years. And he wouldn't start now.

"*Daed*?" Samuel's voice broke through his thoughts. "Who's Sarah Lapp?"

Jacob turned to his son, forcing a smile. "She's... an old friend of the *familye*. She used to work at her parents' bakery here in town."

"Does she make better cinnamon rolls than you?" Samuel asked, his eyes wide with curiosity.

Jacob chuckled despite himself. "*Nee, sohn*. Nobody makes better cinnamon rolls than we do. That's the Zook specialty!"

After Mrs. Yoder left with her payment and a box of fresh pastries, Jacob called his three employees together. They gathered around the large worktable, flour-dusted aprons, and expectant faces turned towards him. The twin Bontrager sisters worked part-time, while Eli Smucker worked one morning a week and each weekday after school.

"I'm sure you've all heard by now but if not," Jacob began, his voice low and serious. "King's Sweet Blessings is reopening."

A murmur ran through the small group. Jacob held up a hand for silence.

"We've worked hard to make this bakery the success it is," he continued. "I don't want anyone to panic. But we need to be prepared for some... changes in business."

"Are you worried, boss?" young Eli asked, his brow furrowed. "I remember those danishes they used to sell."

Jacob paused, choosing his words carefully. "Concerned, maybe. Not worried. We have loyal customers, and our quality speaks for itself. But we can't afford to be complacent."

He outlined his plan: extended hours, a few new specialty items, and perhaps even some holiday promotions. As he spoke, Jacob felt a familiar fire igniting in his chest.

He'd built this bakery from the ground up, turning his modest shop into a thriving business. He wasn't about to let it falter now.

As the employees dispersed back to their tasks, Samuel tugged at Jacob's apron. "*Daed*? Will Sarah Lapp's *dochder* be in my class at school?"

Jacob blinked, caught off guard by the question. That's right, Sarah's daughter was surely of school age. "I... I'm not sure, Samuel. I would imagine so. Why do you ask?"

Samuel shrugged. "Just wondering. It might be nice to have a new friend."

Jacob's heart clenched in response to his son's innocent words. He'd been so focused on the business aspect of Sarah's return that he hadn't considered the personal implications.

How would it affect Samuel to have Sarah reopening the bakery? Would his extra focus on the business come at the expense of his son?

The morning rush began, and Jacob threw himself into his work with renewed vigor. He greeted each customer with a warm smile, making sure every order was perfect. But even as he worked, his mind kept drifting to the modest building across the street, its windows still dark but promising new life.

During a lull in customers, Jacob found himself at the front window, gazing across at King's Sweet Blessings. He could almost see Sarah there, her golden hair tucked neatly under her *kapp*, flour on her cheeks as she kneaded dough. The image was so vivid, it made his chest ache.

"Everything okay, boss?" Eli's voice startled him out of his reverie.

Jacob turned, nodding briskly. "*Jah*, just thinking."

Eli hesitated, then said, "You know, my *Mamm* always says competition is *gut* for business. Keeps us on our toes."

Jacob managed a smile. "Your *Mamm* is a wise woman, Eli."

As the young man returned to his tasks, Jacob's gaze drifted back to the window. Eli's words echoed in his mind, mingling with memories of his own father's teachings. The Amish way was one of community, of supporting one another. But it was also one of hard work and pride in one's craft.

How could he balance those ideals now, with Sarah's return threatening everything he'd built?

The afternoon brought an unexpected visitor in the form of Mr. Anderson, an *Englisch* businessman from the neighboring town. Jacob greeted him warmly, curious about the purpose of his visit.

"Jacob, my friend," Mr. Anderson said, shaking his hand heartily. "I've got an opportunity I think you'll be interested in."

Jacob raised an eyebrow, gesturing for the man to continue.

"There's a big Christmas party being planned for some corporate bigwigs," Mr. Anderson explained. "They're looking for a local bakery to provide all the desserts. It's a substantial contract, Jacob. And I'm sure it would open doors for future catering options, too. It could really put your bakery on the map, even beyond Maple Creek!"

Jacob's pulse quickened at the prospect. A contract like that could secure his bakery's future, providing for his family and employees for months to come. It was exactly the kind of opportunity he needed to stay ahead of the competition.

But even as excitement coursed through him, a nagging doubt took root in his mind. Would pursuing such a large *Englisch* contract be in line with his values?

"It's a generous offer," Jacob said carefully. "When would you need an answer?"

Mr. Anderson grinned. "Take a few days to think it over. But don't wait too long! An opportunity like this won't come around again soon."

Once the *Englisch* businessman had left, Jacob found himself once again at the window, his gaze fixed on King's Sweet Blessings. The "Closed" sign still hung in the window, but he could see movement inside now. Sarah was there, preparing to reopen.

Jacob's hand drifted to his pocket, where he kept his father's old pocket watch. He pulled it out, running his thumb over the worn silver case. His father had always told him that time was a gift from *Gott*, to be used wisely and with purpose.

Now, as the second hand ticked steadily onward, Jacob was torn. Should he bid for the contract, securing his bakery's future but potentially pushing the boundaries of his own conscience? Or should he step back, trusting in *Gott's* plan and the strength of the community to support both his bakery and Sarah's?

The dilemma pressed down on him, as heavy as the dough he'd kneaded that morning. As he tucked the watch back into his pocket, Jacob resolved to pray; hard.

He had some serious soul-searching to do. And with Sarah's bakery set to open any day now, time was not on his side.

"*Daed*?" Samuel's voice broke through his thoughts once again. "Can we make something special for Sarah Lapp and her *dochder*? To welcome them back?"

Jacob looked down at his son, struck by the innocent kindness in his request. For a moment, he saw the situation through Samuel's eyes, not as a threat, but as an opportunity for friendship and community.

"That's a *Wunderbar* idea, Samuel," Jacob said softly, ruffling his son's hair. "Why don't we think about what we could make for them?"

As Samuel eagerly began listing possibilities, Jacob felt some of the tension leave his shoulders. Whatever was coming, he would face it with faith, integrity, and the love of his family. And perhaps, he thought with a glimmer of hope, there might be room in Maple Creek for two thriving bakeries after all.

But as the day wore on and closing time approached, the nagging worry in the pit of his stomach only increased. The Christmas contract loomed large in his mind, a tempting solution to his fears about competition.

While he began preparing to close up shop, wiping down counters and tallying the day's receipts, Jacob sighed. When he turned the key in the lock, flipping the sign to "Closed" for the night, his eyes once again drifted to King's Sweet Blessings across the street. In the fading light, he could just make out the figure still moving inside. Sarah was no doubt working late into the evening to prepare for her grand reopening.

He had little time to make up his mind about the contract. But as he climbed into his buggy, Jacob wondered: what would tomorrow bring for Zook's Bakery? And for his relationship with Sarah Lapp?

Chapter 3

H eart pounding, Sarah reached for the key. The worn brass felt heavy in her palm, a tangible reminder of the responsibility she was about to shoulder.

With a deep breath, she slid the metal into the lock of King's Sweet Blessings and turned it. The familiar click echoed in the pre-dawn stillness, sending a shiver down her spine.

"It's really happening," she whispered to herself, pushing the door open. The scent of yeast and sugar enveloped her, stirring memories of happier times.

Behind her, Emma fidgeted, her small hand clasped tightly in Sarah's. "Can I help, *Mamm*?" she asked, her voice a mix of excitement and sleepiness.

Dear Emma. Her *dochder* refused to let her *mamm* open without her, despite the early hour.

Sarah smiled down at her daughter, love and determination filling her up in equal measure. "Of course, *Liebling*. You can help me turn on the lights."

Together, they stepped into the darkened bakery. Sarah fumbled for the switch, and suddenly the room was bathed in a warm glow. Maple Creek was quite progressive compared with most Amish communities, and although homes didn't have electricity, many businesses did. Emma gasped, her eyes wide as she took in the gleaming counters and freshly painted walls.

"It's so pretty, *Mamm!*" she exclaimed. She danced and twirled with arms extended like a spinning top.

Sarah nodded, blinking back tears. She'd spent every spare moment of the past week scrubbing, painting, and preparing.

Now, seeing it through Emma's eyes, she was glad. "It is, isn't it? This was your *Grossmammi* and *Grossdaadi's* bakery for many years. Now it's ours."

Emma's brow furrowed. "But what about Zook's Bakery across the street? Will they be mad that there's another bakery again?"

Sarah's stomach clenched at the mention of Jacob Zook. She forced a smile.

"*Nee*, Emma. There's room enough for both of us in Maple Creek. Now, let's get you ready for school while the oven warms up."

As Sarah helped Emma into her plain blue dress and neatly tied her prayer *kapp*, her mind raced with all the tasks ahead.

The first batches of bread needed to be in the oven soon if they were to be ready for the morning rush. After they finished baking, she still had to frost the cinnamon rolls, arrange the display case, double check the cash register, not to mention-

"*Mamm?*" Emma's voice broke through her thoughts. "Are you scared?"

Sarah paused, meeting her daughter's earnest gaze. "A little," she admitted. "But that's okay. Sometimes being scared means you're doing something important."

Emma nodded solemnly. "I'm a little scared too. What if the other *kinner* don't like me?"

Sarah's heart ached at the vulnerability in her daughter's voice. She knelt, cupping Emma's face in her hands. "Oh, *Liebling*. They're going to love you. You're kind and smart and funny. Just be yourself, and you'll make friends in no time."

As Emma's face brightened, Sarah sent up a silent prayer, asking for strength and guidance for both of them. *Gott* brought them back to Maple Creek, and she was sure He would keep guiding them now that they were here.

The next few hours passed in a blur of flour and sugar. Sarah moved with practiced efficiency, kneading dough, and sliding trays into the old oven.

She'd forgotten how temperamental it could be, burning the first batch of cookies and underbaking a few loaves of bread, using the back of the appliance. But slowly, the familiar rhythm returned, and the bakery filled with the mouthwatering aroma of fresh baked goods.

Just before seven, Sarah flipped the sign on the door to "Open." She'd gone for limited hours to start, despite the pressing need for funds. Zook's Bakery had been open for an hour already, and she'd seen a steady stream of customers, despite the early hour.

Her heart pounded as she went back to the counter and waited, wondering if anyone would come. Had the community forgotten about King's Sweet Blessings in the years she'd been gone?

The bell above the door chimed, startling her. Mrs. Yoder bustled in, her face lighting up at the sight of Sarah behind the counter.

"*Ach*, Sarah! It's so *gut* to see you back where you belong," she exclaimed, enveloping Sarah in a warm hug. "I'll take a dozen of your famous snickerdoodles and a loaf of sourdough, please."

Sarah's eyes stung with tears of gratitude as she filled the order. "*Danki*, Mrs. Yoder. You're our first customer since reopening. It means so much to have your support."

After Mrs. Yoder left, more customers began to trickle in. Old faces and new, all curious to see what Sarah had to offer. She greeted each one with a smile, even as anxiety gnawed at her stomach.

Would it be enough? Could she really make this work?

Before she knew it, it was time to walk Emma to school. Sarah hastily wiped the flour from her hands and called to her daughter. "Ready, Emma?"

Emma emerged from the back room, her face a mixture of excitement and nerves. "I think so, *Mamm*."

She flipped the sign on the front door and locked it, indicating she'd return in less than thirty minutes. Once Emma was more comfortable, Sarah was confident she'd be fine to walk to school alone, or with one of the other *kinner*.

As they walked down the quiet street, Sarah's mind was still half in the bakery. Had she remembered to turn down the oven? Were there enough napkins stocked?

She shook her head, forcing herself to focus on Emma.

"Remember, *Liebling*," she said softly as they approached the schoolhouse. "Just be yourself. And if you need anything, your teacher knows how to reach me at the bakery. I included the landline number in your lunchbox, too. Just in case."

Emma nodded, squeezing Sarah's hand tightly. As they reached the schoolyard, Sarah spotted the familiar face of Samuel Zook, Jacob's son. She'd seen him with his *daed*, coming and going to and from the bakery.

Little Samuel was always smiling and looked to be a happy little boy. Even now, he was surrounded by a group of children, all laughing at something he'd said.

Sarah's heart clenched. Would Emma be welcomed into that group? Or would Jacob's business rivalry with her extend to their children?

But before she could worry further, Samuel looked up and spotted them. To Sarah's surprise, he broke away from his friends and jogged over.

"*Hallo*, Mrs. Lapp!" he called cheerfully. "Is this your *dochder*?"

Sarah nodded, touched by the boy's friendliness. "*Jah*, this is Emma. Emma, this is Samuel Zook."

Emma smiled shyly. "*Hallo*, Samuel."

"Do you want to *kumm* meet my friends?" Samuel asked, gesturing to the group behind him. "We were just talking about the new reading books Teacher brought in."

Emma's face lit up. She looked up at Sarah, silently asking permission.

"Go on," Sarah encouraged, her heart filled with relief. "I'll see you after school, *Liebling*."

As Emma scampered off with Samuel, Sarah blinked back tears. She watched for a moment as the children welcomed Emma into their circle, their laughter carrying across the schoolyard.

With a deep breath, Sarah turned and headed back to the bakery. There was still so much to do but knowing that Emma was settling in eased some of the weight on her shoulders.

The rest of the morning passed in a whirlwind of customers and baking. Sarah barely had time to catch her breath, let alone worry about competition or finances. It wasn't until the lunch rush began to die down that she overheard a conversation that made her pause.

"Did you hear about that big *Englischer* contract?" Mrs. Stoltzfus was saying to Mrs. Beiler while they sipped their coffee. "I heard Mr. Anderson say it's worth thousands and thousands of dollars to whoever wins the bid. They have one for the dinner catering and one for the desserts."

Sarah's ears perked up as she pretended to wipe down the counter nearby.

Mrs. Beiler nodded. "*Jah*, I heard Elizabeth Troyer is thinking of bidding for the dinner contract. It could really put Maple Creek on the map."

"But isn't it awfully worldly?" Mrs. Stoltzfus asked, lowering her voice. "All those fancy *Englischers*..."

Their voices faded as they moved away, but Sarah's mind was racing. A contract worth thousands? That might well be the answer to all her problems. The answer to her prayers.

With that kind of money, she could pay off her parents' debts, maybe even upgrade the bakery's equipment, or set aside some savings for the future.

But was it right? Would pursuing such a large, worldly contract go against her values? It was for an *Englischer* Christmas party...

She considered what they might want to be made for dessert. An image of Santa Claus cookies crossed her mind and Sarah winced. Maple Creek was progressive, but they were still Amish.

Perhaps not. But if they let her pick the items, or were open to compromising on the designs...

Sarah pushed the thoughts aside when another customer approached the counter. She'd have to consider it later when she had time to think clearly. To think through it all in detail.

The afternoon flew by. Before Sarah knew it, it was time to close up shop and pick up Emma from school.

As she flipped the sign to "Closed," she exhaled, a tired glow of accomplishment making her smile. She made it through the first day.

It wasn't perfect, of course - a few burnt loaves after the morning's issues with undercooking, not to mention that dropped tray of muffins...

But overall? It was a successful day.

As Sarah approached the schoolhouse, her heart lightened at the sight of Emma's beaming face. Her daughter came running, the loose ties of her prayer *kapp* streaming behind her.

"Mamm! Mamm!" Emma called. "I had the best day ever!"

Sarah laughed, scooping Emma into a hug. "Did you now? Tell me all about it."

As they walked home, Emma chattered excitedly about her new friends, the books they'd read, and how the teacher praised her arithmetic skills. Sarah listened, her heart full of gratitude. At least Emma was happy and settling in well.

But as Emma's chatter died down, Sarah's mind returned to the overheard conversation. The vendor contract loomed large in her thoughts, a tempting solution to her financial worries.

Could she really consider bidding? And if she did, how would it affect her standing in the community?

She'd only just returned. Would bidding on an *Englischer* Christmas contract be frowned upon by the district? Would they stop coming to her bakery?

As they reached the bakery, Sarah paused with her hand on the door. Through the window, she could see the empty display cases and envision the stack of bills filling the cash register.

The day's earnings were good, but not nearly enough to make a dent in their debts, especially as she planned to use most of it to pay for more supplies. To keep the bakery open longer, she needed more products to sell.

At least her *daed* would be able to come by and help out every once in a while, so she didn't need to worry about hiring. An employee, even part-time, would eat up even more of their limited funds.

"Mamm?" Emma's voice broke through her thoughts. "Are you okay?"

Sarah forced a smile. "Jah, Liebling. Just thinking about tomorrow's baking."

But as they entered the quiet bakery, Sarah knew she had a big decision to make. The vendor contract could be the lifeline they needed - or it could be a step too far into the *Englisch* world. As she began to prepare for the next day, Sarah sent up a silent prayer for guidance.

Tomorrow would bring new challenges, but for now, Sarah allowed herself a moment of hope. They'd made it through the first day.

And with *Gott's* help, she would keep fighting to save the bakery and support her family - vendor contract or not.

Chapter 4

Jacob's arms strained under the weight of the wooden crate as he maneuvered through the bustling market. The crisp December air nipped at his cheeks, carrying the mingled scents of fresh produce, baked goods, and wood smoke.

He'd barely slept the night before, his mind racing with thoughts of new recipes and marketing strategies. Now, as he dodged around chattering customers and overflowing stalls, he forced himself to focus on the task at hand.

"*Daed*!" Samuel's excited voice piped up from somewhere behind him. "Can I help carry something?"

Jacob glanced over his shoulder, a small smile tugging at his lips despite his preoccupation. "*Nee*, Samuel. I've got it. Just make sure you don't lose that box of-"

His words were cut short as he collided with something solid. The crate tipped precariously, and Jacob's heart leaped into his throat. With lightning-fast reflexes, he managed to steady it, but not before two cinnamon rolls tumbled to the ground.

"Oh!" a soft, feminine voice exclaimed. "I'm so sorry! I wasn't looking where I was going."

Jacob looked up, ready to brush off the apology, but the words died on his lips. Standing before him, cheeks flushed with embarrassment, was Sarah Lapp.

For a moment, Jacob couldn't speak. He'd known she was back in town, of course - it had been the talk of Maple Creek for the last week.

And he'd seen her through the window, in her bakery, even in the street...

But seeing her here, in the flesh, was something else entirely.

Her golden hair peeked out from beneath her *kapp*, and her warm brown eyes were wide with concern. She looked... *gut*. Healthy. Happy, even.

Jacob swallowed hard, forcing himself back to reality. "It's fine," he managed, his voice gruffer than he'd intended. "No harm done."

Sarah bent down, quickly retrieving the fallen cinnamon rolls. "Oh, but your beautiful pastries! I'm so sorry, Jacob. I'll pay for them, of course."

The sound of his name on her lips sent an unexpected jolt through him. How long had it been since they'd spoken? Since before she'd left town, surely.

Before she married. Before...

Before.

Jacob shook his head, both to clear his thoughts and to refuse her offer. "*Nee*, it's not necessary. It is just a couple of rolls."

"*Daed*!" Samuel's voice broke through the awkward moment. "Look who I found!"

Jacob turned to see his son standing with a young girl, her blonde hair in neat braids beneath her *kapp*. Emma Lapp.

He'd seen her around town, too, but never up close. The resemblance to Sarah was striking.

"*Hallo*, Mr. Zook," Emma said shyly, her small hand clasped in Samuel's. "Samuel was just telling me about your cinnamon star bread. It sounds *wunderbar*."

Jacob felt a surge of pride, both at his son's friendliness and at Emma's interest in their baking.

"*Danki*, Emma. It's nice to meet you properly."

Sarah smiled, her eyes softening as she looked at the children. "Emma's been so excited to try all the different foods at the market. It's her first time here."

"Really?" Samuel's eyes widened. "But it's the best! *Daed*, can I show Emma our stall? Please?"

Jacob hesitated, glancing at Sarah.

She nodded, her smile widening. "If it's all right with your *Daed*, Emma would love that."

"*Jah*, go ahead," Jacob relented. "But be careful, and don't touch anything without asking first."

The children scampered off and Jacob found himself alone with Sarah. The initial awkwardness returned, hanging heavy in the air between them.

"So," Sarah said, breaking the silence. "H-how have you been, Jacob? The bakery looks to be doing well."

Jacob nodded, adjusting his grip on the crate. "*Jah*, we've been blessed. And you? I hear you've reopened King's Sweet Blessings."

A flicker of something - pride? determination? - passed across Sarah's face.

She lifted her chin a little, almost as if she was daring him to do... something. Or at least, that's how he took it.

"That's right. It's been a challenge, but a *gut* one. The community has been so supportive."

Jacob's mouth tasted sour. Was it jealousy? Concern? He wasn't sure.

"That's... *gut*," he said, the words stiff on his tongue. "Maple Creek has always been a close-knit community."

Sarah's eyes met his, and for a moment, Jacob felt as if she could see right through him. "It has," she agreed softly. "I'd forgotten how much I missed that."

Before Jacob could respond, a customer approached Sarah's makeshift stall.

"Mrs. Lapp!" the older woman called. "I heard you were back! Do you have any of those wonderful apple strudels today?"

Sarah's face lit up. "*Jah*, Mrs. Yoder! I made a fresh batch this morning. Let me get one for you."

Sarah turned to help her customer, and Jacob found himself watching her. Her movements were graceful and efficient, and her smile was warm and genuine as she chatted with Mrs. Yoder.

It was clear she hadn't lost her touch with people; or with baking if the delighted expression on Mrs. Yoder's face was any indication.

Jacob felt a conflicting mix of emotions churning in his gut. On the one hand, Sarah's skill and charm were undeniable.

She was clearly a formidable competitor, one who could potentially threaten his bakery's success. But on the other hand, seeing her in her element, happy and confident, stirred something in him that he couldn't quite name.

Or maybe he just didn't want to name it.

"Jacob?" Sarah's voice pulled him from his thoughts. She was looking at him curiously, a small basket in her hands. "I wanted to give you these as an apology for the cinnamon rolls. And... well, as a peace offering, I suppose."

Jacob blinked, surprised. In the basket were several perfectly formed sugar cookies, decorated with intricate designs in white icing. "Sarah, you don't have to-"

"I want to," she interrupted gently. "I know my return has probably caused some... complications for you. But I hope we can find a way to coexist peacefully. Maybe even help each other sometimes."

Jacob stared at the basket and then at Sarah. Her expression was open, honest. There was no hint of deception or ulterior motive in her warm brown eyes.

For a moment, he was transported back in time to when they were younger, and life was simpler. Before life sent them in such very different directions.

"*Danki*," he said finally, accepting the basket. "They lo ok... *wunderbar*."

Sarah's smile widened, revealing those charming dimples he'd never quite forgotten about. "I hope you enjoy them. And Jacob... I'm glad we had a chance to talk. Even if it started with me nearly knocking you over."

Despite himself, Jacob felt the corners of his mouth turning up. "*Jah*, well. Maybe next time we can skip the collision part."

Sarah laughed, the sound light and musical. "Deal. I should get back to my stall, but... it was *gut* to see you, Jacob. Truly."

As she walked away, Jacob found himself watching her go, the basket of cookies still in his hands. He wasn't sure what to make of this encounter.

Sarah was still his competitor, still a potential threat to his business. But she was also... Sarah.

The girl he'd grown up with, the woman who'd left and come back changed but somehow still the same. At least, in the ways that mattered.

"*Daed*!" Samuel's voice broke through his musings. "Emma says her *Mamm* makes the best snickerdoodles ever. But I told her yours are better. Can we have one to compare?"

Jacob looked down at his son and then across the market to where Sarah was arranging her display. She caught his eye and gave a small wave, which he found himself returning before he could think better of it.

"We'll see, Samuel," he said, ruffling his son's hair. "For now, let's focus on our stall. We have customers waiting."

As they settled into the rhythm of the market day, Jacob remained unsettled. Something had shifted, but what?

Sarah King Lapp was back in Maple Creek, and she was clearly here to stay. What that meant for him, for his bakery, for the community... well, only time would tell.

But as he bit into one of Sarah's sugar cookies later that morning, savoring the perfect balance of sweetness and richness, Jacob had to admit - at least to himself - that having her back in town might not be such a bad thing after all.

The market bustled around him, a cacophony of voices and laughter. Jacob found his gaze drawn again and again to Sarah's stall, watching as she charmed customer after customer with her warm smile and delectable treats. He watched the steady stream of people gravitating towards her, many of them his own regular customers.

"Did you hear?" a woman whispered loudly to her friend as they passed Jacob's stall. "Sarah Lapp's apple danishes are just like I remember from when I was a girl. It's like her *Mamm* is back in the kitchen!"

Her companion nodded enthusiastically. "*Ach, jah,* and those cinnamon rolls! I bought a dozen. My little Ezra won't eat anyone else's now. Though I still prefer Zook's myself."

Jacob felt a twinge of unease. He'd known Sarah would be popular - nostalgia was a powerful draw, after all. But hearing his own customers praise her baking so effusively ... it was more than a little concerning.

"*Daed*?" Samuel's voice broke through his thoughts. "Can I go talk to Emma again? She wants to show me her *Mamm's* sugar sculptures."

Jacob blinked, pulled from his worries. "Sugar sculptures?"

Samuel nodded eagerly. "*Jah*! Emma says her *Mamm* makes these amazing things out of sugar. Animals and flowers and even little houses! Can I go see?"

Jacob hesitated. Part of him wanted to say no, to keep his son - and himself - firmly separated from the Lapps and their bakery.

But the excited gleam in Samuel's eyes was hard to resist. And if he was being honest with himself, he was curious too.

"All right," he relented. "But just for a few minutes. We've got work to do here."

As Samuel scampered off, Jacob's gaze kept drifting towards Sarah's stall. He told himself it was just to keep an eye on Samuel, but deep down, he knew there was more to it than that.

Finally, after a few minutes, he gave up and asked his neighbor to watch over his stall. His feet took him directly to his competitor's stall.

Sarah was in the middle of explaining her sugar sculptures to a small crowd when Jacob approached. Her eyes lit up when she saw him, her expression a mix of surprise and pleasure.

"Jacob! I'm so glad you came over," she said warmly. "I was just telling everyone about my newest creation. It's a miniature version of the Maple Creek schoolhouse."

Jacob's eyes widened as he took in the intricate sugar sculpture. Every detail was perfect, from the tiny bell in the tower to the miniature slate boards visible through the windows. It was, he had to admit, incredibly impressive.

"It's... remarkable," he said, unable to keep the awe from his voice. "I've never seen anything like it."

Sarah beamed, her cheeks flushing slightly at the praise. "*Danki*, Jacob. It's a technique I learned while I was away. I-I knew how to make basic ones before, but I learned from a master craftsman in Lancaster. I thought it might be a nice addition to our offerings at King's Sweet Blessings."

Jacob nodded, his mind racing. Sugar sculptures weren't something he'd ever considered for his own bakery. They were beautiful, certainly, but were they practical? Would they sell? And yet, looking at the crowd gathered around Sarah's stall, he couldn't deny their appeal.

"They're *wunderbar, Mamm!*" Emma exclaimed, her eyes wide with admiration. "Can you teach me how to make them someday?"

Sarah laughed, ruffling her daughter's hair affectionately. "Of course, *Liebling*. When you're a bit older, we'll start with something simple."

Jacob watched the interaction, a strange ache forming in his chest. He'd always prided himself on being a *gut* father to Samuel, but seeing Sarah with Emma... there was a warmth there, a closeness that he sometimes felt he lacked with his son.

Maybe, it was simply a mother's natural bond and warmth. His heart ached.

Abigail...

"Mr. Zook?" Emma's voice pulled him from his thoughts. "Do you think the sugar sculptures are pretty?"

Jacob met the little girl's earnest gaze, so like her mother's. "*Jah*, Emma. They're very pretty indeed."

Emma's face lit up. "Maybe you could make some for your bakery too! Then both you and *Mamm* would have the prettiest treats in all of Maple Creek!"

Jacob swallowed, a rush of conflicting emotions swirling behind his sternum at Emma's innocent suggestion. The idea of copying Sarah's idea didn't sit well with him, but the thought of falling behind, of losing customers to her unique offerings...

"That's very sweet of you to suggest, Emma," Sarah said gently, casting an apologetic glance at Jacob. "But I think Mr. Zook's bakery is plenty special just as it is. Isn't that right, Jacob?"

Jacob cleared his throat, oddly touched by Sarah's words. "*Jah*, that's right. We each have our own specialties."

Although, he'd always prided himself on cinnamon rolls. And he'd heard at least one customer explicitly say her son preferred Sarah's to his.

Was it just a matter of taste? Or was even his best work inferior to hers?

As the crowd began to disperse, Jacob lingered a few moments longer. He watched as Sarah expertly wrapped up pastries for customers, her movements quick and efficient. There was a grace to her work, a joy that was evident in every interaction.

"You seem to be settling in well," he found himself saying as the last customer walked away.

Sarah looked up, surprise flickering across her face. "Oh! I didn't realize you were still there, I'm sorry." She laughed, tucking a wayward strand of hair behind her ear, and looking away. Was she nervous? "*Jah*, I suppose I am. It's been... challenging but rewarding too. The community has been so welcoming."

Jacob nodded, unsure of what to say next. Part of him wanted to warn her off, to say something unkind, imply that Maple Creek didn't need two bakeries; although really, he was the newcomer.

But another part... another part was curious. Intrigued, even.

"Your sugar sculptures," he said finally. "They're truly impressive. I've never seen anything like them around here."

Sarah's face softened. "*Danki*, Jacob. That means a lot, coming from you. I know you've become the baker to beat in Maple Creek. That's what my *daed* said, anyway." She smiled at him, as sweet as her sugar sculptures.

Her words sent an unexpected thrill through him. She saw him as competition, as someone to measure herself against. It was both flattering and unsettling.

"Well," he said, struggling to maintain his composure, "I suppose we'll both have to bring our best to the table now."

Sarah's eyes met his and for a moment, Jacob felt as if he could see right into her soul. There was determination there, yes, but also a warmth, a kindness that he'd almost forgotten.

"I look forward to it," she said softly. "A little healthy competition can bring out the best in all of us, don't you think?"

Before Jacob could respond, Samuel came bounding up, Emma close behind. "*Daed*! Can Emma come to our stall? I want to show her something!"

Jacob glanced at Sarah, who nodded her approval. "*Jah*, Samuel. But just for a few minutes, remember? We have work to do."

As the children scampered off, Jacob found himself lingering once more. He knew he should get back to his own stall, but something kept him rooted to the spot.

"Jacob," Sarah said, her voice low and serious. "I want you to know... I'm not here to cause trouble. I'm just trying to make a life for Emma and myself. To carry on my *familye's* legacy."

Jacob met her gaze, surprised by the intensity he found there. "I understand," he said and was surprised to realize he meant it. "We all have to do what's best for our families."

Sarah nodded, relief evident in her expression. "*Danki* for understanding. And Jacob... I hope that maybe, in time, we can be friends again. Like-like we used to be."

As she turned back to her work, Jacob stood frozen in place, her words echoing in his mind. Friends.

The idea was appealing, certainly. It was also frightening. Could they really go back to how things were before?

Did he even want to?

Walking back to his own stall, Jacob's mind was a whirlwind of conflicting thoughts and emotions. Sarah Lapp was more than just a competitor. He had to accept that, even if he didn't want to.

She was a piece of his past and a current complication in his carefully ordered life. What part she might play in his future, he had no idea.

He turned and looked back at her one more time, and the baker in him watched her interact with customers, her smile bright and her laughter infectious, Jacob couldn't help but wonder: What did Sarah Lapp's return *really* mean for Maple Creek? For his bakery? For him?

Chapter 5

Sarah's hands trembled as she slid the tray of Lebkuchen into the temperamental oven. The rich aroma of honey, molasses, and spices filled the air, mingling with the ever-present scent of yeast and sugar that permeated King's Sweet Blessings.

She held her breath, silently praying that this batch would turn out perfectly. It had to be perfect. Her future - Emma's future - depended on it.

As she closed the oven door, a familiar groaning caught her attention. Sarah froze, her heart sinking. Not again. Please, not now.

"*Mamm*!" Emma's voice rang out as the bell above the bakery door chimed. "I'm back from school!"

Sarah forced a smile, pushing aside her worries as she turned to greet her daughter. "*Hallo, Liebling*! How was your day?"

Emma's face was flushed with excitement as she bound into the kitchen, her blue eyes sparkling. "It was *wunderbar*! We learned about different animals, and Samuel helped me draw some of them. Look!"

As Emma proudly displayed her artwork, Sarah felt both joy and guilt wash over her. She loved seeing her daughter so happy and engaged in school, but the mention of Samuel Zook sent a pang through her heart.

How would Jacob react if he knew their children were becoming fast friends? Oh, he'd seen them interact at the market, and their interactions were frankly warmer than she hoped.

But a single day's interaction was one thing. An ongoing friendship was another.

After all, she and Jacob were fast friends as children... though, Emma and Samuel's bond was more sibling-like, by Sarah's reckoning.

"That's beautiful, Emma," Sarah said, admiring the colorful drawing. "You and Samuel did a *gut* job."

Emma beamed, her smile as bright as the sun in her drawing. "Can I help you bake, *Mamm*? Please?"

Sarah hesitated, glancing at the temperamental oven. She had so much work to do and with the oven acting up again... But the hopeful look in Emma's eyes was impossible to resist.

"Of course, *Liebling*," she relented. "Why don't you start by measuring out the ingredients for the next batch of Lebkuchen? You remember the recipe, *jah*?"

Emma nodded eagerly, already reaching for her small apron. As she bustled around the kitchen, carefully measuring flour and spices, Sarah watched with a surge of pride.

Her daughter was growing up so fast, already showing a keen interest in baking. Just like Sarah had at her age.

The oven creaked again, drawing Sarah's attention back to the present. She approached it warily, peering through the cloudy glass.

The Lebkuchen inside were rising nicely, their surfaces beginning to crack in that perfect, rustic way her *mamm's* always had. But lately, the oven's temperature was fluctuating wildly, threatening to ruin all her hard work.

"Steady," Sarah murmured as if the oven could hear her. "Just a few more minutes."

"*Mamm*?" Emma's voice was hesitant. "Is something wrong with the oven again?"

Sarah sighed, turning to face her daughter. There was no use hiding it. Emma was perceptive, and she'd been around the bakery enough to know when things weren't right.

"*Jah, Liebling,*" Sarah admitted. "It's being a bit... temperamental today."

Emma's brow furrowed in concern. "Can we fix it?"

Sarah felt a lump form in her throat. If only it were that simple. The oven was old - ancient, really. It had been in the bakery since her *Grossmammi's* time. Replacing it would cost more money than they had, but repairing it was becoming increasingly difficult and expensive.

"We'll figure something out," Sarah said, forcing confidence into her voice. "For now, let's focus on making the best Lebkuchen anyone in Maple Creek has ever tasted. Can you hand me the powdered sugar, please?"

As they worked side by side, Sarah's mind wandered to the vendor contract. Mr. Anderson stopped in at her bakery just yesterday, and after one bite of her apple danish, told her about the contract and suggested she put a proposal together.

He confirmed the compensation, and Sarah did her best to hide how tempting that was. The opportunity to provide desserts for the big *Englischer* Christmas party could do so much for the bakery. For her family.

The money from that contract could solve so many problems - it could pay for a new oven, cover their debts, a maybe even allow them to expand the bakery's offerings.

But was it right? Would pursuing such a large, worldly contract go against her values? Visions of Santa Claus cookies danced through her mind again. She grimaced, stomach churning.

She should've asked Mr. Anderson what limitations or expectations they had for the contract.

"*Mamm*!" Emma's alarmed voice snapped Sarah back to reality. "The oven!"

Sarah whirled around, her heart racing. Smoke was seeping out of the oven, filling the kitchen with an acrid stench.

She rushed forward, yanking open the door. A wave of heat hit her face as she peered inside, her heart sinking at the sight of the blackened Lebkuchen.

"*Ach, nee*," she murmured, fighting back tears of frustration. All that work, all that time... all those precious ingredients, wasted.

"It's okay, *Mamm*," Emma said, her small hand slipping into Sarah's. "We can make more, *jah*?"

Sarah looked down at her daughter, struck by the determination in those blue eyes so like her own. She managed a small smile, squeezing Emma's hand. "*Jah, Liebling*. We can make more."

Together, they salvaged what they could of the ruined batch, setting aside the few cookies that were only slightly overcooked. While they mixed up a new batch, Sarah found herself relaxing into the familiar rhythm of baking, studiously ignoring the implications of the oven disaster.

The last time the temperature fluctuated like that, it was just one batch. Then it worked just fine afterward.

So, surely it would be the same this time. It had to be. Emma chattered away about her day at school, her excitement infectious.

"Samuel says his *Daed* is thinking about making gingerbread houses for Christmas," Emma said as she carefully spooned dough onto a baking sheet. "Maybe even a whole village! Can we make some too, *Mamm*?"

Sarah paused, her hand hovering over the bowl of spices. Gingerbread houses. Of course Jacob would be making those. His elaborate creations had always been a highlight of the Maple Creek Christmas market.

"Maybe," Sarah said noncommittally. "We'll see how busy we are."

As the afternoon wore on, Sarah's thoughts kept drifting back to the vendor contract. The pros and cons warred in her mind, each seemingly outweighing the other at every turn. The money would be heaven-sent, allowing them to upgrade equipment and pay off debts. But the potential backlash from the community, the strain it might put on her business if the members of their district disapproved...

Could she really afford that?

But then, could she afford not to even try?

"*Mamm*?" Emma's voice broke through her thoughts. "Can I decorate some of the Lebkuchen? Like we did last Christmas?"

Sarah blinked, realizing she'd been standing idle, lost in thought. "Of course, *Liebling*. Let me get the icing ready."

They worked on decorating the baked goods, and Sarah relaxed a little. This was what mattered, she reminded herself.

These moments with Emma, carrying on her family's baking traditions. The vendor contract, any and all competition with Zook's Bakery - all of that paled in comparison to the joy of creating something beautiful with her daughter.

"Look, *Mamm*!" Emma held up a Lebkuchen she'd decorated with a simple but elegant snowflake design. "Do you think it's *gut* enough to sell?"

Sarah's heart swelled with pride. "It's beautiful, Emma. I think it might be the prettiest one in the whole batch."

Emma beamed, carefully setting it aside. "Maybe we can make special ones for the big *Englisch* feast. With fancy designs and everything!"

Sarah froze, her piping bag hovering over a half-decorated cookie. "The *Englisch* feast?" she asked, trying to keep her voice casual. "What do you know about that, *Liebling*?"

Emma shrugged, reaching for another cookie to decorate. "I heard Mrs. Yoder talking about it when she came in yesterday. She said it could be a big deal for the bakery. Is that true, *Mamm*?"

Sarah set down her piping bag, taking a deep breath. She'd been so caught up in her own thoughts, she hadn't considered how the potential contract might affect Emma.

"It could be," she said carefully. "But it's complicated, *Liebling*. There's a lot to consider."

Emma looked up, her blue eyes serious. "Is it because of Mr. Zook's bakery? Samuel says his *Daed* is always worried about competition."

Sarah felt a pang in her chest. Was that how Jacob saw her? As nothing more than competition?

"It's not just about that," she said. "It's... well, it's about finding the right balance. Between our traditions and the need to support our *familye* and our community."

Emma nodded solemnly, though Sarah wasn't sure how much she truly understood. "I think you should do it, *Mamm*," she said after a moment. "Your Lebkuchen are the best in the whole world. The *Englischers* would love them."

Sarah couldn't help but smile at her daughter's unwavering faith in her. "*Danki, Liebling*. We'll see what happens."

As the day wound down and the last customers left the bakery, Sarah was left alone with her thoughts once more.

Emma was upstairs, getting ready for bed, and the bakery was quiet save for the occasional creak of the cooling oven.

Sarah moved through the kitchen, tidying up and taking stock of what they'd accomplished that day. Despite the setbacks with the oven, they'd managed to produce a respectable amount of Lebkuchen, along with their usual array of bread and pastries.

But would it be enough?

Her eyes fell on the small stack of bills tucked away on her desk. The numbers loomed large in her mind, a constant reminder of their precarious financial situation.

And then there was Emma to think about, her schooling, her future. Sarah wanted to give her daughter every opportunity and provide her with the stable, loving home she deserved.

Sarah's gaze drifted to the window and then beyond to the lights of Jacob's bakery across the street. Was he facing the same dilemma? Did he lie awake at night, worrying about the future of his business, his family?

With a sigh, Sarah reached for a piece of paper and a pencil. She began to list the pros and cons of bidding for the vendor contract, just as her father had taught her to do when faced with a difficult decision.

On one side, the potential financial benefits, the opportunity to showcase her baking to a wider audience, and the chance to secure a more stable future for Emma. On the other, the risk of alienating her community, of straying too far from her values...

As she wrote, Sarah's resolve strengthened. This wasn't just about her; it was not even just about Emma. It was about honoring her family's legacy, about keeping King's Sweet Blessings alive and thriving for years to come.

"*Mamm*?" Emma's voice called from upstairs. "Can you *kumm* tuck me in?"

"Coming, *Liebling*!" Sarah called back, setting down her pencil. She climbed the stairs to Emma's room, her heart full of love for this precious child who had become her whole world.

Emma was already in bed, her favorite quilt pulled up to her chin. "Will you sing me a song, *Mamm*?" she asked sleepily.

Sarah smiled, sitting on the edge of the bed. As she began to sing a soft hymn, her hand stroked Emma's hair absently.

Fully present, everything else fell away: the worries about the bakery, the vendor contract, the competition with Jacob. All that mattered was this, her daughter, safe and loved.

As Emma drifted off to sleep, Sarah leaned down and kissed her forehead. "*Ich liebe dich, mein Schatz*," she whispered. She crept out of the room, looking at her daughter one last time before closing the door as softly as she could.

Back downstairs, Sarah stood in the quiet bakery, her decision made. She would bid for the vendor contract.

It wouldn't be easy, and it might ruffle some feathers in the community. But for Emma, for her family's legacy, for the future of King's Sweet Blessings, she had to try.

Sarah picked up her pencil again, this time to begin drafting her bid. As she worked, she sent up a silent prayer, asking for guidance and strength in the days to come.

Gott brought her this far. He would be with her as she moved forward with the bid, too.

But as she wrote, a nagging thought tugged at the back of her mind. How would Jacob react when he learned of her decision? Did he know about the contract, too? Was he planning a bid?

She didn't want to drive a further wedge between them. Sarah still hoped to rekindle their friendship, and if they ended up competing for a lucrative contract, surely that would destroy any hope of reviving that bond for the future.

She bit her lip. Better not to stir the pot.

Only time would tell. But for now, Sarah had cookies to bake and a contract to win.

Chapter 6

His brow furrowed, deep in concentration, Jacob breathed. With steady hands, he moved to carefully attach another gingerbread wall to the growing structure before him.

The scent of cinnamon and molasses filled the air, mingling with the ever-present aroma of fresh bread that permeated Zook's Bakery. He paused, scrutinizing his work with a critical eye.

This year's Gingerbread Village had to be perfect. It wasn't just a Christmas display anymore; it was his bid for the coveted vendor contract through Mr. Anderson. The contract that would ensure the future of his bakery.

The bell above the door chimed and Jacob looked up to see Samuel bounding in, his cheeks flushed from the cold air outside.

"*Daed*! I'm here to help!" his son called out, already shrugging off his coat. The little boy grinned up at his father.

Jacob had to smile at Samuel's enthusiasm. "*Gut*. Wash your hands first, then you can start on decorating the cookies."

Knowing his son as he did, Jacob prepared a sheet of sugar cookies for the lad to decorate. Normally, he might not fret over Samuel helping with the gingerbread decorations, but not this year.

As Samuel scampered off to the sink, Jacob returned his attention to the gingerbread village. He'd always prided himself on his baking skills, but this December, there was extra pressure.

A lot of it.

The vendor contract loomed in his mind, a tantalizing opportunity that could secure his bakery's future. And yet...

"*Daed*?" Samuel's voice broke through his thoughts. "Is this the right amount of icing?"

Jacob looked over, nodding approvingly. "*Jah*, that's perfect. Remember to hold the piping bag steady as you work."

As they worked side by side, Jacob found himself relaxing into the familiar rhythm of baking. Samuel chattered away about his day at school, his excitement infectious.

"Emma showed me how to make a paper snowflake today," Samuel said, carefully placing a dollop of icing on the next cookie. "She's really *gut* at it. Her *Mamm* taught her."

Jacob's hands stilled for a moment at the mention of Sarah. "Is that so?" he managed, keeping his voice neutral.

Samuel nodded enthusiastically. "*Jah*! Emma says her *Mamm* can make all sorts of pretty things. With paper *and* sugar!"

Jacob felt a twinge in his chest. He'd seen Sarah's sugar sculptures at the farmers' market. They were undeniably impressive. "That's... nice," he said, struggling to find the right words.

The bell chimed again, and Mrs. Yoder bustled in, her arms laden with shopping bags. "*Guder Mariye*, Jacob!" she called cheerfully. "Oh my, is that this year's gingerbread village? It's coming along beautifully!"

Jacob straightened, wiping his hands on his apron. "*Danki*, Mrs. Yoder. What can I get for you today?"

As he helped Mrs. Yoder with her order, Jacob tensed as he overheard her conversation with another customer who had just entered.

"Did you try Sarah Lapp's apple strudel yet?" Mrs. Yoder was saying. "It's just like I remember from when we were girls and her *mamm* made it. Melts in your mouth!"

The other woman nodded enthusiastically. "Oh *jah*, and those cinnamon rolls! Just like I remembered." She shook her head. "I bought a dozen last week and they were excellent. But my David still prefers Zook's, so here I am."

Jacob felt a knot form in his stomach. He'd known Sarah would be popular - nostalgia was a powerful draw, after all. But hearing his own customers praise her baking so effusively... was more than a little concerning.

As the women left, still chattering about Sarah's baking prowess, Jacob found himself staring at the half-finished gingerbread village. Suddenly, it looked completely inadequate. Utterly plain. Perfectly ordinary.

Not good enough by far.

"*Daed*?" Samuel's voice pulled him from his thoughts. "Are you okay?"

Jacob blinked, forcing a smile. "*Jah*, just thinking. How about we add some more details to the village? Maybe some trees and lampposts? Can you help me make those?"

Something like a lamppost ought to be well within his son's abilities. Jacob could always tweak them, if needed.

Samuel's face lit up. "Can we make a tiny sleigh, too?"

Jacob nodded, already reaching for more gingerbread dough. "Why not? Let's make this the best gingerbread village Maple Creek has ever seen."

As they worked, Jacob's mind raced. He'd always been a little too competitive, but this felt different.

It wasn't just about business anymore. Otherwise, he could laugh off the customer comments and focus solely on improving his cinnamon rolls so that everyone preferred them.

After all, Sarah wasn't just another baker - she was... Sarah.

He started adding intricate details he'd never bothered with before: delicate icing icicles hanging from rooftops, tiny wreaths on doors. Each addition was one more declaration of how serious he was about winning the contract. He'd push the limits of his skills and beyond.

"Wow, *Daed*," Samuel breathed, stepping back to admire their work. "It's amazing!"

Jacob surveyed the village critically. It was undoubtedly his best work yet. But was it enough?

The afternoon wore on, with a steady stream of customers coming and going. Jacob greeted each one with his usual warmth, but that nagging worry in the back of his mind popped up again and again.

Every praise of his baking was met with an internal comparison to Sarah's. Every mention of the upcoming Christmas season reminded him of the contract.

If only he'd just... accepted as soon as Mr. Anderson mentioned it. Maybe then he wouldn't have these worries.

But now, he waited too long and the *Englischer* decided to take bids for it. Would Mr. Anderson choose Jacob's?

As closing time approached, Jacob drifted over to the front window, staring across at King's Sweet Blessings. The lights were still on. He frowned.

He squinted. Was Sarah working late?

The rival bakery closed hours ago. So why was she still there?

A conflicting swirl churned in Jacob's gut. Admiration for Sarah's dedication. Respect for her skill. And yes, a twinge of jealousy at the ease with which she seemed to have won over the community.

"*Daed*?" Samuel's voice broke through his thoughts. "Can we add some more snow to the village? I think it needs more sparkle."

Jacob turned back to his son, struck by the innocence in his request. For a moment, he saw the situation through Samuel's eyes, not as a competition, but as an opportunity to create something beautiful.

"That's a wonderful idea, Samuel," Jacob said softly, ruffling his son's hair. "Let's make it sparkle."

As they added more detailed touches to the gingerbread village, some of the tension dropped from Jacob's shoulders. He would face the challenges ahead, but for now, he could enjoy this time with his son.

But as he locked the bakery that night, his eyes once again drifted to King's. Sarah was still there, her silhouette visible through the window as she worked on what looked like an intricate sugar sculpture.

Jacob's resolve hardened. He respected Sarah, admired her even.

But this was business. And he had a bakery to run and a son to provide for.

Tomorrow, he decided he would brainstorm how to make his official bid for the vendor contract even better. He'd pull out all the stops and showcase every skill he possessed. The gingerbread village was just the beginning.

As he climbed into his buggy, Jacob tried to ignore the teetering feeling in his chest. Like standing on the precipice of something momentous.

The vendor contract, his rivalry with Sarah, the future of his bakery - it all seemed to be coming to a head.

He welcomed the obstacles. Maple Creek wasn't ready for what he had in store. And neither, he suspected, was Sarah Lapp.

The sound of the horse's hooves echoed in the quiet street as Jacob headed home, a sleepy Samuel by his side. His mind was already whirling with plans for tomorrow. The real competition was just beginning, and Jacob Zook intended to win.

But as he glanced one last time at Sarah's bakery, a small voice in the back of his mind whispered a question he wasn't quite ready to address: Was winning really what he wanted? Or was there something - or someone - more important at stake?

Jacob pushed the thought aside, focusing on the road ahead. Tomorrow would bring new challenges and new opportunities. And he would face them head-on, just as he always had.

But for now, he had a son to tuck in and prayers to say; prayers that, despite his best efforts, couldn't help but include a certain brown-eyed baker across the street.

Chapter 7

S arah panicked, her breath coming in short, staccato gasps. Her fingers trembled as she frantically turned the knobs on the ancient oven, heart pounding in her chest.

"*Kumm* on, *kumm* on," she muttered, her voice tinged with desperation. The oven remained stubbornly cold, its inner workings as silent as a graveyard.

"*Nee, nee, nee,*" Sarah whispered, fighting back tears. "Not now. Please, not *now.*"

She yanked open the oven door, peering inside as if sheer willpower could bring it back to life. The empty cavity mocked her, its cold interior a dark reminder of just how precarious her situation was.

Sarah slumped against the counter, her mind racing. Her parents were out of town, otherwise she was certain *Daed* could help. They'd gone to a big hospital out of town for her *mamm's* latest round of treatment and tests.

How would she bake tomorrow's items to sell? Maybe she could find someone to barter with for repairs, but how long would that take?

And without a working oven, how could she possibly complete her bid for the vendor contract? She'd spent all of last night thinking about her bid while idly making a sugar sculpture late into the evening.

But now, with this new setback?

The crush of responsibility - to Emma, to her parents, to the legacy of King's Sweet Blessings - pressed down on her, threatening to crush her entirely.

The bell above the door chimed, startling Sarah from her spiral of despair. She quickly wiped her eyes, forcing a smile as she turned to greet the customer. She ought to close early. But instead of a friendly face, she was met with the concerned gaze of her daughter.

"*Mamm*?" Emma's voice was small, her blue eyes wide with worry. "What's wrong?"

Sarah's heart clenched. She hated seeing that look on her daughter's face, knowing she was the cause.

"It's nothing, *Liebling*," she said, trying to keep her voice steady. "Just a small problem with the oven. Nothing to worry about."

Emma's brow furrowed, unconvinced. She set her schoolbooks on the counter and moved closer, peering at the stubborn appliance. "Is it broken again?"

Sarah sighed, running a hand through her hair. There was no use hiding the truth from her perceptive daughter. "*Jah*, I'm afraid so. But don't worry, I'll figure something out."

Emma's face scrunched up in thought, a look Sarah knew all too well. It was the same expression she wore when tackling a particularly challenging math problem. Probably, an expression Sarah herself wore when creating new recipes.

"What if..." Emma began hesitantly. "What if we asked Mr. Zook for help?"

Sarah blinked, taken aback by the suggestion. "Mr. Zook? *Jacob* Zook?"

Emma nodded eagerly. "*Jah!* Samuel says his *daed* can fix anything. Maybe he could help with our oven?"

Sarah's stomach twisted at the thought of asking Jacob for help. They were competitors, after all. And their his tory... well, that was complicated enough without adding this to the mix.

"I don't think that's a *gut* idea, Emma," she said gently. "Mr. Zook has his own bakery to run. We can't bother him with our problems."

But Emma was undeterred. "I could ask Samuel at school tomorrow," she pressed. "He wouldn't mind, I'm sure of it!"

Sarah opened her mouth to protest further, but the determined gleam in Emma's eyes gave her pause. Her daughter's sometimes stubborn faith in the goodness of others was both heartwarming and, in this case, a bit exasperating.

"Let's not worry about that now," Sarah said, forcing a smile. "How about you tell me about your day at school while I see if I can figure this out?"

As Emma chattered away about her lessons and friends, Sarah turned back to the oven, her mind whirling. She should discourage Emma from involving the Zooks, but a small, desperate part of her immediately latched on to that glimmer of hope.

What if Jacob could help? What if this was the answer to her prayers?

Sarah shook her head, pushing the thought aside. No, she couldn't rely on Jacob Zook. Even if he *could* help, that certainly didn't mean he *would*.

And anyway, she'd got this far on her own, and she would find a way through this too. She had to.

The next day found Sarah elbow-deep in dough, kneading furiously as if she could work out all her frustrations through the simple act of baking. She'd managed to borrow a small countertop oven from an *Englisch* regular who came in just before closing time, but it was woefully inadequate for the bakery's needs. Thank *gutness* her bakery had electricity, otherwise she'd be entirely out of business until the gas oven was fixed.

Still, she refused to give up. She'd stayed up half the night, recalculating recipes and adjusting baking times to make the most with what she had.

The bell above the door chimed and Sarah called out a distracted greeting, not bothering to look up from her work. It wasn't until she heard the familiar deep voice that her head snapped up, her hands stilling in the dough.

"*Hallo*, Sarah," Jacob Zook said, his tall frame filling the doorway.

Sarah blinked, certain she must be hallucinating from lack of sleep. But no, Jacob was really there, standing in her bakery with a toolbox in hand and an unreadable expression on his face.

"Jacob," she managed, her voice squeaking up half an octave to betray her surprise. "What are you doing here?"

He shifted uncomfortably, his eyes darting around the bakery before settling back on her. "I, uh... I heard you might be having some trouble with your oven. Samuel mentioned that Emma was worried."

Sarah's cheeks flushed with embarrassment. Of course, Emma had gone ahead and asked Samuel, despite her attempts to dissuade her.

"*Ach*, I... That's very kind of you, but we're fine. Really. You didn't need to *kumm* all this way."

Jacob quirked an eyebrow, a touch of humor on his handsome face. "All the way from across the street?"

"Ah, *jah*," she stammered.

His gaze fell on the small countertop oven that was clearly struggling to keep up with even the limited menu she'd cut back on for the day. Bread and simple cookies, with nary a danish in sight.

He looked at her, steady and warmer than she expected. "Are you sure about that?"

Sarah's shoulders slumped, the fight draining out of her. What was the point in pretending?

"*Nee*," she admitted softly. "We're not fine. The oven... it's completely given up. I-I don't know what to do."

Sarah swallowed, blinking hard. He would *not* see her cry. She clenched her jaw and breathed in slowly through her nose, then exhaled a long breath through her lips.

Something flickered in Jacob's eyes - compassion, perhaps? Or was it pity? Sarah couldn't be sure. She didn't want to know, not right now.

"Let me take a look," he said, already moving towards the kitchen. "I might be able to help."

Sarah hesitated, torn between her desperate need for assistance and her pride. But the thought of disappointing Emma, of letting down her parents and the entire community that depended on King's Sweet Blessings... was too much to bear.

"All right," she said finally. "*Danki*, Jacob. I... I really appreciate this."

While Jacob set to work examining the oven, Sarah busied herself with closing the storefront and setting the dough in the refrigerator to chill. She fought to ignore the strange flutter in her stomach at having him in her kitchen.

It had been so long since they'd been in the same space, working side by side like this. It stirred up memories she'd long tried to suppress.

"So," Jacob's voice broke through her reverie, "how long has it been acting up?"

Sarah sighed, leaning against the counter. "Since I got back, if I'm being honest. But I kept hoping it would hold out just a little longer. We've been so busy with the holiday rush, and then there's the..." She trailed off, realizing she'd nearly revealed more than she'd intended. She cleared her throat. "There's a lot to do."

Jacob's head popped up from behind the oven, his brow furrowed. "You've been dealing with a temperamental oven since you reopened?" His voice was surprisingly gentle. "It must be hard on top of everything else. But the gut news is, I don't think any customers have noticed. Well," he said, looking at the black cavern. "Not before today. I'm glad Emma came to ask for my help."

Their eyes met, and for a moment, Sarah saw right into Jacob's soul. There was a depth of understanding there, a shared experience that transcended their current roles as competitors.

They were both widowed parents, after all, trying to build a future for their children in a world that sometimes seemed determined to knock them down.

"It's not easy, is it?" Sarah found herself saying, her voice barely above a whisper. "Doing this on your own, I mean."

Jacob's expression softened, and he nodded. "*Nee*, it's not. There are days when I..." he paused, seeming to struggle with his words. "Days when I wonder if I'm doing right by Samuel. If I'm enough."

Sarah's heart clenched at the vulnerability in his admission. "I know exactly what you mean," she said softly. "Sometimes I look at Emma, and I just... I wish I could give her everything she deserves. A stable home, a future without worry."

"You're doing a gut job with her, Sarah," Jacob said, his voice warm with sincerity. "Anyone can see how happy and well-adjusted she is. You should be proud."

Sarah felt tears prick at the corners of her eyes, over-whelmed by Jacob's unexpected kindness. "*Danki*," she managed. "And you... Samuel is a *wunderbar* little boy. You've raised him well."

She knew, from her parents' letters over the years, that Jacob married Abigail Maas less than a year after she and Matthew married. And that he'd lost her years ago, left to raise little Samuel on his own.

Just like she'd lost her Matthew.

A comfortable silence fell between them as Jacob returned to his work on the oven. Sarah found herself watching him, admiring the confident way he handled the tools, and the determined set of his jaw as he tackled each new challenge.

It was strange, she thought, how life could bring you full circle. Here they were again, years later, in a situation neither of them would ever have predicted.

"I think I've found the problem," Jacob announced after what felt like hours. "It's the heating element. It's completely shot."

Sarah's heart sank. "Can it be fixed?"

Jacob hesitated, then nodded slowly. "*Jah*, but it won't be cheap. And it might take a few days to get the part."

Sarah closed her eyes, fighting back a wave of despair. A few days without a proper oven could be disastrous for the bakery. And the cost... she didn't even want to think about how she'd manage that. A problem for another day.

"*Ach*, there now," Jacob's voice was gentle, closer than she expected. She opened her eyes to find him standing right in front of her, his blue eyes filled with concern. "It'll be all right, Sarah. We'll figure something out."

The 'we' in his statement caught her off guard, sending an unexpected warmth through her chest. "We?" she echoed, hardly daring to hope.

Jacob nodded, a small smile tugging at the corners of his mouth. "*Jah*, we. Look, I know we're competitors, but... we're also neighbors. Part of the same community. And more than that, we're..." he trailed off, seeming unsure how to finish the thought.

"*Freinds*?" Sarah supplied, almost plaintive. She was surprised at how much she wanted it to be true.

Jacob's smile widened, reaching his eyes in a way that made Sarah's heart skip a beat. "*Jah, freinds*. So, as your *freind*, I'm telling you - we'll figure this out."

Sarah inhaled, the weight lifting from her shoulders to be replaced by a cautious hope. "*Danki*, Jacob," she said softly. "I don't know how to repay you for this."

He shook his head, his expression serious. "You don't need to repay me, Sarah. Just... just keep making those amazing apple strudels of yours. The world would be a sadder place without them." He gave her a lopsided smile.

Sarah had to laugh at that, the sound bubbling up from deep within her. It was good, she realized, to laugh like this. To feel, even for a moment, like everything really would turn out all right.

Jacob gathered his tools, preparing to leave, and Sarah was reluctant to see him go. There was something comforting about his presence, a steady strength that made her feel... safe. Protected, even.

"Jacob," she called out as he reached the door. He turned, his eyebrows raised in question. "I... *Danki*. For everything."

He nodded, his eyes softening in a way that made Sarah's breath catch. "Anytime, Sarah. I mean that."

As the door closed behind him, Sarah leaned against the counter, her mind whirling. What just happened?

How had Jacob Zook, her business rival, become her unexpected savior? And more importantly, why did the thought of seeing him again make her heart race in a way it hadn't in years? Not since losing Matthew.

Sarah shook her head, trying to clear her thoughts. She had work to do, a bakery to run, a daughter to care for. She couldn't afford to get distracted by... whatever this was.

And yet, as she turned back to her baking, she relished the warmth that settled in her chest. For the first time in a long while, Sarah Lapp felt a glimmer of hope for the future, and it had nothing to do with ovens or vendor contracts.

As she worked, humming softly to herself, Sarah couldn't push aside the lingering questions in her mind.

What would the future bring?

And how would Jacob Zook be a part of it?

Chapter 8

T wo days later, Jacob carefully disassembled the ancient oven, its rusted screws groaning in protest. The familiar scent of yeast and sugar filled his nostrils, mingling with the metallic tang of old machinery. He paused, wiping sweat from his brow, and glanced over his shoulder at Sarah Lapp.

She stood behind the counter, her delicate hands kneading dough with the same intensity he'd seen in her eyes when she'd opened the bakery door. The afternoon sun streaming through the windows caught the loose strands of her golden hair, creating a halo effect that made Jacob's breath catch in his throat.

"How's it looking?" Sarah asked, her voice tinged with worry. "Can you fix it now the part came in?"

Jacob cleared his throat, pushing aside the unexpected flutter in his chest. "It's seen better days," he admitted. "But I think I can get it running again. Might take a while, though."

Sarah's shoulders sagged with relief. "*Danki*, Jacob. I can't tell you how much this means to me."

He nodded, turning back to the oven to hide the flush creeping up his neck. What was he doing here, helping his biggest competitor? And why did her gratitude make him feel so... warm? So happy?

Jacob worked away, Sarah always in sight through the corner of his eye, admiring her dedication. She moved effortlessly around the kitchen, her hands never idle.

Even with a broken oven and nothing but a small electric replacement, she'd whipped up an impressive array of baked goods and breads. The countertops were lined with cooling racks, each one laden with golden-brown delights that made his mouth water.

"*Mamm*!" Emma's excited voice broke through the companionable silence. "Can Samuel and I work on our Christmas quilt project here? Please?"

Jacob looked up to see his son standing beside Sarah's daughter, both children's eyes shining with anticipation. Sarah hesitated, glancing at Jacob.

"Is that all right with you?" she asked softly.

Jacob found himself nodding before he could think better of it. "*Jah*, of course. Just stay out of the way of the oven, *kinner*. It's not safe right now."

The children settled at a small table near the window, and Jacob returned to his task. But his mind kept wandering, distracted by the easy chatter between Emma and Samuel.

"Your *Mamm's* sugar sculptures are amazing," Samuel was saying. "Do you think she could teach me how to make them someday?"

Emma's face lit up with pride. "Oh, *jah! Mamm's* the best at sugar sculptures. She says it's like painting with sugar. Maybe we could all learn together!"

Jacob's heart twisted with... Jealousy? Admiration? He wasn't sure.

He'd seen Sarah's sugar sculptures at the farmer's market and behind the counter. They were indeed impressive. But hearing his son's enthusiasm for learning from her stirred up conflicting emotions. Didn't Samuel want to learn from *him*?

"Jacob?" Sarah's voice pulled him from his thoughts. She stood beside him, a steaming mug in her hands. "I thought you might like some *kaffe*. It's rather chilly in here with the oven off. Almost a nice change from boiling even in winter," she added with a laugh.

He accepted the mug gratefully, their fingers brushing for the briefest moment. He ignored the desire to let his fingertips linger on hers.

"*Danki*," he murmured, taking a sip. The rich, bold flavor surprised him. "This is *gut*. Really *gut*."

Sarah smiled, and Jacob's chest filled with that unexpected warmth again. "It was my late husband's favorite blend," she said softly. "I still make it every day, even th ough..."

She trailed off, her eyes misting over. Jacob felt a surge of empathy. He knew all too well the pain of loss, the empty space left behind by a beloved spouse.

"I understand," he said, his voice low. "My Abigail... she used to bake these little cinnamon rolls every Sunday morning. I haven't been able to make them since she passed, only the big ones. I just... can't."

Sarah nodded, her eyes meeting his. For a moment, Jacob felt as if she could see right into his soul. "It's the little things that catch you off guard the most, isn't it?" she said softly.

Jacob swallowed hard, suddenly aware of how close they were standing. He could see the flecks of gold in Sarah's warm brown eyes, and smell the faint scent of vanilla that clung to her skin like perfume.

"*Jah*," he said, a little hoarse. "It is."

They stood in silence for a moment, the shared understanding of loss hanging between them. Then, from across the room, Emma's voice broke the spell.

"*Mamm*! Look what Samuel showed me how to do!"

Jacob stepped back, clearing his throat. "I should, uh... I should get back to work on the oven," he said, gesturing awkwardly with his coffee mug.

Sarah nodded, a faint blush coloring her cheeks. "Of course. Let me know if you need anything else."

While she returned to her baking, Jacob threw himself back into the task at hand. But again and again, his gaze was pulled back to the lovely baker at work. He stole glances at Sarah as she worked, admiring the graceful way she moved, the gentle smile she wore as she kneaded dough, the easy rapport she had with both *kinner*...

One hour, then another passed, filled with the rhythmic sounds of Jacob's tinkering and Sarah's baking. The children's chatter provided a pleasant background noise, punctuated occasionally by bursts of laughter.

Despite the circumstances, Jacob was enjoying the afternoon more than he cared to admit. It was a *gut* thing he had employees to cover his shop, although he hadn't told them just how he was spending the afternoon.

Finally, as the sun began to dip low in the sky, Jacob stood up with a triumphant grin. "I think that should do it," he announced. "Let's give it a try."

Sarah hurried over, hope and anxiety warring on her face. Jacob flipped the switch, and they both held their breath. For a moment, nothing happened. Then, with a low hum, the oven sprang to life, slowly releasing heat into its cavernous belly.

"Oh, Jacob!" Sarah exclaimed, her eyes shining. "You did it!"

Before he knew what was happening, Sarah had thrown her arms around him in a grateful hug. Jacob froze, momentarily stunned by the warmth of her embrace. Then, hesitantly, he returned the hug, his large hands resting gently on her back.

"It was nothing," he mumbled, acutely aware of how well she fit against him. "Just a simple part swap and some cleaning."

Sarah pulled back as if she'd touched a hot stove, her cheeks flushed. "Ach, I-I'm so sorry." She stepped back, looking anywhere but his face. "But it wasn't nothing," she insisted. "You've saved my bakery. Please, how can I repay you for the time and effort?"

Jacob shook his head, surprising himself with these words. "*Nee*, that's not necessary. We're... we're neighbors. It's what neighbors do."

Sarah's eyes widened, a mix of gratitude and confusion playing across her face. "But... we're competitors," she said softly. "Why would you just help me like this?"

Jacob found himself at a loss for words. Why had he helped her? It went against every business instinct he had. And yet, looking at Sarah's earnest expression, he didn't regret it.

Not one bit.

"Because it was the right thing to do," he said finally. "And because... because maybe we don't have to be just competitors."

The words hung in the air between them, heavy with possibility. Sarah's lips parted slightly as if she wanted to say something but couldn't find the words.

"*Daed*?" Samuel's voice broke the moment. "Can we stay for supper? Mrs. Lapp invited us earlier when you were working!"

Jacob blinked, pulled back to reality. He glanced at Sarah, who blinked as if she'd forgotten the off-the-cuff invitation. But then, she nodded vigorously.

"It's the least I can do," she said. "Especially if you won't take any payment. Supper, to thank you for your help."

Against his better judgment, Jacob agreed. As they settled around Sarah's small kitchen table above the bakery, the aroma of freshly baked bread and hearty stew filling the air, he worried, a little.

Was he crossing a line? She'd hugged him earlier... and he hugged her back. And now, supper?

But watching Samuel and Emma chattering away, seeing the genuine warmth in Sarah's smile as she served the meal, all Jacob felt was... rightness. Comfort and peace.

The conversation flowed easily, punctuated by laughter and stories. Jacob relaxed, drawn in by Sarah's quick wit and gentle teasing. He couldn't remember the last time he'd enjoyed a meal this much, the last time he'd felt so... at home.

As the evening drew to a close, Jacob helped Sarah clear the table. Their hands brushed as they reached for the same plate, sending an unexpected jolt through him. He looked up, meeting Sarah's gaze and for a moment, his breath and the world stopped.

"Jacob," Sarah said softly, her eyes searching his. "*Danki*. Truly"

He swallowed hard, suddenly aware of how close they were standing. Again.

"You're welcome," he said, his voice rough. "I'm glad I could help."

Something unspoken passed between them, a current of understanding and connection that left Jacob breathless. Sarah felt it too, didn't she?

She must. He should step back, gather Samuel, and leave. But he was rooted to the spot, captivated by the warmth and possibilities he saw in Sarah's eyes.

The moment was broken by the sound of Samuel and Emma laughing in the other room. Jacob blinked, reality crashing back in.

What was he doing? This was Sarah Lapp, his competitor. The woman whose success could threaten everything he'd built.

And yet... as he said his goodbyes, as he watched Sarah stand in the doorway waving as he and Samuel climbed into their buggy, Jacob's mind ricocheted from moment to moment, like an *Englischer* film.

Her hand brushing his as she gave him her husband's favorite coffee blend... the bright hope he and Samuel would stay for dinner, and after dinner...

His mouth went dry. He'd come to fix an oven, but he'd left with... what, exactly?

Confusion.

Uncertainty.

Yearning for that soft peace, that utter rightness and sense of being exactly where he should be, sitting at her table.

Peace.

Home.

As they drove through the quiet streets of Maple Creek, Samuel's excited chatter fading into the background, Jacob was more lost than ever. He'd helped a competitor today, had enjoyed her company, and felt a connection he hadn't experienced in years.

What did it all mean? And more importantly, what was he going to do about it?

Chapter 9

With her head bowed in prayer, Sarah let the familiar rhythms of the Sunday service wash over her. The wooden pew creaked beneath her as she shifted, her mind struggling to focus on Bishop Stoltzfus's sermon. Instead, her thoughts kept drifting to the vendor contract, to the mounting bills on her desk, to the future of King's Sweet Blessings.

To Jacob Zook.

"*Mein Gott*," she whispered, mouthing the words more than speaking them so her voice was not even audible even to herself, "please guide me as You always have. Show me the path You would have me take. How do we overcome the obstacles ahead of us?"

A small hand slipped into hers, and Sarah opened her eyes to see Emma looking up at her, concern etched on her young face. Sarah managed a small smile, squeezing her daughter's hand reassuringly. She had to be strong, for Emma's sake if nothing else.

As the service drew to a close, Sarah's gaze wandered to the far side of the room where Jacob Zook sat with his son, Samuel. Jacob's broad shoulders were straight, his attention fixed on the bishop.

But as if sensing her eyes on him, he turned slightly, meeting her gaze for a brief moment. He nodded, once.

Sarah's cheeks flushed at being caught and she quickly looked away without nodding back. Mentally, she chastised herself for the traitorous flutter in her stomach.

The congregation began to file outside, the frigid air filled with the soft murmur of greetings and well wishes and goodbyes. Sarah held Emma's hand as they made their way towards the door, nodding and smiling at her neighbors.

"Sarah," a deep voice called from behind her. She turned to see Jacob approaching, Samuel in tow. "*Guder mariye.*"

"*Guder mariye*, Jacob," Sarah replied, acutely aware of the curious glances from those around them. It wasn't often that the owners of Maple Creek's two bakeries were seen in friendly conversation. "I hope you're well?"

Jacob nodded, his eyes warm despite the slight awkwardness in his stance. "*Jah, danki.* And you? How's the bakery? The oven?"

Sarah hesitated, unsure how much to reveal. "It's.. . much better," she said finally. "The oven's working perfectly now, thanks to you."

And if the bill for the heating element she had to buy on credit sat on her office desk, well. He'd already helped them more than she ever expected.

It was only one of a half dozen bills, anyway. Some with bright red "Overdue" stamps already on them.

A ghost of a smile played at Jacob's lips. "*Gut* to hear. If you need any more help, just let me know."

Before Sarah could respond, Emma tugged at her skirt. "*Mamm*, can Samuel *kumm* over to work on our Christmas project for school?"

Sarah glanced at Jacob, who looked as surprised as she felt. "Oh, I don't know, *Liebling*. I'm sure Mr. Zook has plans with his *sohn* today..."

"Actually," Jacob interjected, his voice surprisingly gentle, "we don't have anything pressing. If it's not an impos ition..."

Sarah found herself nodding before she could think better of it. "Of course not. You're both welcome to join us for a meal, if you'd like."

As they walked home to the bakery, Emma skipping ahead with Samuel, Sarah fretted. What had she just gotten herself into?

Having Jacob in her home, sharing yet another meal... it was dangerously close to something she wasn't ready to name. At least this time, they'd stay downstairs in the bakery, where there was room for the children to spread out and work on... whatever it was they were doing.

Her Emma was tight-lipped about it, refusing to give her *mamm* even a hint. Likely, she'd try to banish her *mamm* to the kitchen to keep it secret. But Sarah didn't mind indulging her daughter one bit.

Seeing Emma smile again, after those first awful months without Matthew... it was worth anything.

Worth everything.

The afternoon passed in a blur of activity. While the children worked on their secret Christmas project, Sarah, laughing as she was exiled, busied herself in the kitchen.

Jacob was apparently allowed in on the secret and stayed with the *kinner*. She ignored the way her pulse quickened every time Jacob's deep laugh drifted in from the other room.

Or tried to, at least.

Sarah put extra care into the meal, selecting ingredients with care and adding a touch more cinnamon to the apple pie than usual.

When they sat down to eat a little later, Sarah was struck by how... right it felt. Emma and Samuel's chatter filled the air, punctuated by Jacob's thoughtful questions and quiet chuckles. It was as if he belonged there, at her table, in her home.

In her heart?

"This is delicious, Sarah," Jacob said, helping himself to another slice of pie. "I can see why your bakery's doing so well."

Sarah ducked her head, at the compliment. She mumbled, "*Danki*, Jacob. It's just a simple recipe..."

"*Nee*, it's more than that," he insisted, his eyes meeting hers. "You have a real gift."

The intensity of his gaze made Sarah's heart skip a beat. She looked away, flustered, only to catch Emma watching them with a bright smile.

Sarah cleared her throat, standing abruptly. "Who's ready to help clean up?"

As they worked together to clear the table and wash the dishes, Sarah relaxed into the easy rhythm of conversation with Jacob. They talked about their childhoods in Maple Creek, shared funny stories about their children, and even cautiously broached the subject of their late spouses.

"It's hard, *jah*?" Jacob said softly as he dried a plate. "Raising a child alone, running a business... Either one by itself is a lot, but both?"

Sarah nodded, her throat tight with unexpected emotion. "*Jah*, it's not easy. But we do what we must, for their sake, *jah*?"

Jacob's hand brushed against hers as he reached for another dish, sending a jolt of electricity through her. She inhaled a sharp breath.

He didn't seem to notice.

"*Jah*, we do. But, Sarah... you don't have to do it all alone. If you ever need help, or just someone to talk to..."

Sarah looked up, meeting his gaze. The warmth and sincerity she saw there made her breath catch. "*Danki*, Jacob," she managed. "The same goes for you, you know."

The moment stretched between them. She was frozen, lost in his soft gaze.

It was Emma's voice that finally broke the spell. "*Mamm*! Can we show you and Mr. Zook our project now?"

Sarah turned away and gave a shaky laugh. "*Ach*, so now I'm allowed to see the big secret?"

"*Jah*! It's ready now," Emma said with a giggle as she ran in. Her daughter grabbed Sarah's hand and dragged her to the other room.

As the children proudly displayed their handmade Christmas ornaments, Sarah fought to keep her mind from wandering. She couldn't deny the growing connection between her and Jacob, and the way her heart seemed to lighten in his presence.

But was it right to pursue these feelings? She hardly had time for her daughter and the bakery... and speaking of the business...

They were competitors, after all. Not to mention the work she had left for the vendor contract.

The thought of the contract snapped Sarah back to reality. She still had so much work to do on her bid. "*Ach*, I hate to cut this short," she said, glancing at the clock, "but I have something I need to finish up."

It was the Sabbath, but surely *Gott* understood the deadline she was under. He would forgive ceding to the pressure this one time, right?

Jacob nodded, understanding in his eyes. "Of course. Samuel, time to head home."

As they said their goodbyes at the door, Sarah lingered, despite the mountain of work waiting for her. "*Danki* for coming," she said softly. "It was... nice."

Jacob smiled, and Sarah's heart did that odd little flip again. "It was," he agreed. "Perhaps we will do it again sometime."

She nodded, mute.

After they left, Sarah hurried to the bakery's kitchen, pushing thoughts of Jacob to the back of her mind. She had a contract to win, a future to secure for herself and Emma. There was no time for... whatever this was with Jacob Zook.

Hours passed as Sarah pored over her bid proposal, tweaking recipes, and crunching numbers. The bakery was quiet save for the scratch of her pencil and the occasional creak of the old building settling. Thank goodness Emma was old enough to entertain herself in their small apartment above the bakery. Outside, the sky darkened, stars appearing one by one in the velvet expanse.

Sarah rubbed her eyes, fatigue setting in. But she couldn't stop now.

This contract could be the answer to all her prayers. She could pay off the debts and get the bakery's finances back into the black.

As she worked, Sarah found Jacob's soft smile and warm gaze pop into her mind more than once. What would he think of her bid?

Would he be proud of her determination, or see her as a threat to his own business? The thought of competing directly with him made her stomach churn. The bid was open to anyone who cared to enter, but why would he? Zook's was established, and beloved by the people of Maple Creek.

Like King's Sweet Blessings had been, once upon a time.

"Focus, Sarah," she muttered to herself, shaking her head. She couldn't afford to let her growing feelings for Jacob distract her from what was truly important.

Finally, as the clock chimed midnight, Sarah sat back with a sigh of relief. Her bid was complete, every detail accounted for. She'd poured her heart and soul into this proposal, showcasing not just her baking skills but her dedication to quality and tradition.

She'd stayed true to her values, with nary a Santa Claus cookie to be found.

Sarah closed her eyes, offering up one last prayer. "*Mein Gott*," she whispered, "I've done all I can. Please let it be enough."

With trembling hands, she sealed the bid in an envelope, her neat handwriting stark against the crisp white paper. Tomorrow, she'd deliver it to Mr. Anderson's office in the neighboring town. But for now, all she could do was wait and hope and pray.

As Sarah took a moment and stepped out into the chilly December night, her breath forming small clouds in the air, she shivered.

Relief and anxiety filled her in equal measure. But she was done, so why was she still so nervous? She'd done her best and put everything she had into this bid. Surely that had to count for something.

Her eyes drifted across the street to Jacob's darkened bakery. Feeling wistful, she imagined a future where they weren't competitors, where they could explore their growing connection without the shadow of business rivalry hanging over their heads.

But that was a fool's dream, at least right now.

Sarah shook her head, pushing the thought aside. There was no use in daydreaming. She had a bakery to run, a daughter to raise, and a community to serve. Whatever happened with the vendor contract - and with Jacob - would happen in *Gott's* own time.

As she walked back inside, the distant stars twinkling overhead, Sarah exhaled, her breath forming a cloud of white vapor that dissipated into nothingness.

She'd done all she could. Now, it was in *Gott's* hands.

Little did Sarah know, across town, Jacob Zook was just putting the finishing touches on his own bid for the very same contract. The stage was set for a competition that would test not just their baking skills, but the fragile connection growing between them.

Chapter 10

J acob cast a hurried glance over his work before moving to apply the final touches to his gingerbread village. He paused, scrutinizing his work with a critical eye. This wasn't just a Christmas display anymore; it was the centerpiece of his bid for the coveted vendor contract through Mr. Anderson.

As he added a delicate swirl of icing to the church steeple, Jacob's mind wandered to Sarah Lapp. Was she working on her own bid right now?

The thought sent an unexpected pang through his chest. He never even mentioned the contract to her, despite his knowledge of her financial woes. What did that say about him?

That he was a shrewd businessman? That he was petty? That he was cold-hearted? That he didn't care about her, about little Emma and their fate?

He shook his head in disgust, refocusing on the task at hand. This contract could secure his bakery's future and provide for Samuel. He couldn't afford to let his growing... whatever it was for Sarah, distract him.

The bell above the door chimed, and Jacob heard rather than saw Samuel bustling indoors. His attention was fixed on the work in front of him.

"*Daed*! I'm home from school!" his son said.

Jacob chuckled at Samuel's enthusiasm. "I can hear that, *sohn*. How was your day?" He finished one more detail and then set the icing bag down, turning to give his son his attention.

Samuel's face fell slightly, and Jacob's paternal instincts kicked in. "What's wrong, *sohn*?"

"*Daed*," Samuel began hesitantly, "why did Timmy Yoder say Emma and I shouldn't be *freinds*?"

Jacob froze, his piping bag hovering over the gingerbread village. He'd known this conversation would come eventually, but he'd hoped to have more time to prepare. "What do you mean, Samuel?"

Samuel fidgeted with the strap of his school bag. "He said that since you and Mrs. Lapp own different bakeries, Emma and I can't be *freinds*. But that doesn't make sense, does it?"

Jacob set down his piping bag, wiping his hands on his apron as he tried to find the right words. "It's... complicated, Samuel. Mrs. Lapp and I, we're... business rivals. Since we both run bakeries, well, we're competing for the same customers."

Even as the words left his mouth, Jacob felt a twinge of guilt. Was that really all Sarah was to him? A rival?

Samuel's brow furrowed in confusion. "But why does that mean Emma and I can't be *freinds*? You were nice to Mrs. Lapp when you fixed her oven. And we ate with them. Twice! I don't understand, *Daed*."

Jacob sighed, running a hand through his beard. "You're right, Samuel. Being business rivals doesn't mean we can't be friendly. It's just... complicated for adults sometimes."

"But why?" Samuel pressed, his eyes wide with innocence. "Mrs. Lapp is nice, and Emma is my *freind*. Why can't we all be *freinds*?"

Jacob felt his resolve wavering under his son's earnest gaze. "It's not that simple, *sohn*. In business, we need to keep our customers. When Mrs. Lapp reopened her bakery, it meant some of our customers might start buying from her instead. He gave his son an awkward smile. "That's why I've been working so hard on this gingerbread village and the contract bid. We need to show that we're the best bakery in Maple Creek."

As he spoke, Jacob realized how hollow his words sounded. Was this really the example he wanted to set for his son?

Samuel's face fell. "So... you don't want me to be *freinds* with Emma?" he asked, eyes round and voice small.

"*Nee*, that's not what I'm saying," Jacob quickly amended, as a surge of guilt stung his heart. "You can be *freinds* with Emma. It's *gut* to be kind to everyone, no matter what."

"Then why can't you and Mrs. Lapp be *freinds* too?" Samuel asked, his voice still small. "I thought... I thought you *were freinds*.

Something in Jacob's chest twisted. He thought of Sarah's warm smile and the way her eyes lit up when she talked about baking.

He remembered the easy conversation they'd shared over dinner, the way she'd understood his struggles as a single parent without him having to explain. The way his heart pounded when their hands touched.

"I... I, well, Samuel," Jacob said, fumbling for the right words. "I suppose maybe we can be."

Samuel nodded solemnly. "Well, I'm going to stay *freinds* with Emma, no matter what. And I hope you and

Mrs. Lapp can be *freinds* too, *Daed*. She makes you smile more."

With that, Samuel headed upstairs to do his homework, leaving Jacob alone with his thoughts. He stared at the gingerbread village, suddenly seeing it in a new light.

Was this truly what *Gott* wanted from him? To push so hard for success that he risked alienating a good woman and her daughter? Not to mention, what lessons was he teaching his son?

Jacob's mind drifted to Sarah's situation. He *knew* she was struggling to keep her bakery afloat and to provide for Emma on her own. Wasn't that exactly what he was doing for Samuel? How could he fault her for trying to succeed?

With a heavy sigh, Jacob made his way to the small office where he worked on business ledgers. He needed guidance, and there was only one place he knew to turn. Pulling his well-worn Bible from the reading stand, Jacob sat at his desk and began to flip through the pages.

His eyes fell on a familiar verse in Proverbs: "A generous person will prosper; whoever refreshes others will be refreshed."

Jacob paused, letting the words sink in. Was his competitive drive truly in line with *Gott's* teachings? Or was there a better way?

He read on, finding comfort in verses about compassion and kindness. As the evening light faded outside, Jacob felt a shift in his heart. Maybe there was room in Maple Creek for two extremely successful bakeries. Maybe he and Sarah could find a way to coexist, to support each other even as they ran separate businesses.

The thought scared him. It would mean letting go of old habits, of the fierce competitiveness that had driven him for so long.

But as he closed his Bible, an ease filled Jacob's chest. He didn't have all the answers yet, but his faith in *Gott* was steadfast.

Jacob stood, stretching his tired muscles. He had a lot to think about, and even more to pray over. But for now, he had a son to feed and a gingerbread village to finalize.

As he made his way back to the kitchen, Jacob's eyes fell on the contract bid sitting on the counter. He picked it up, weighing it in his hands.

Tomorrow, he'd have to deliver it to Mr. Anderson's office. But, tonight... tonight he had some serious soul-searching to do.

"Samuel!" he called up the stairs. "*Kumm* help me clean up. Then we'll have supper and maybe take a walk."

Jacob heard the excited patter of his son's feet overhead and smiled. At the very least, he had to set a better example for Samuel. And maybe, that example included finding a way to work alongside Sarah Lapp instead of against her.

As Samuel bounded down the stairs, Jacob ruffled his hair affectionately. "Tell me more about your day at school," he said. "And about Emma. She seems like a *gut freind* for you."

Samuel's face lit up, and he launched into a detailed account of their latest project. Jacob listened, embracing the warmth spreading through his chest. It was like sitting in front of a cast iron stove after coming in from the cold. He might not have all the answers yet, but now, thanks to his son, he was on the right path.

Later that night, as Jacob tucked Samuel into bed, his son's sleepy voice caught him off guard.

"*Daed*? Do you think Mrs. Lapp likes you?"

Jacob felt his ears burn. "What makes you ask that, Samuel?"

"Well," Samuel yawned, "Emma says her *mamm* smiles more when she talks about you. And you smile more when you talk about Mrs. Lapp. So I thought maybe you like each other."

Jacob's heart skipped a beat. "It's... complicated, *sohn*. For now, Mrs. Lapp and I are maybe just *freinds*. Now, time for sleep. *Gute Nacht*."

After he closed Samuel's door, Jacob leaned against the wall, his mind whirling. Did Sarah really smile more when she talked about him? And was it that obvious that he... felt something for her? So obvious that mere *kinner* picked up on it?

Jacob made his way downstairs, restless. He paced for a half hour, then decided to take a short walk outside. Just to clear his mind.

The achingly clear skies and cold air did little to calm the whirling thoughts in his mind, but it did at least tire his body. Jacob prepared for bed, his mind whirled with thoughts of the coming days.

The vendor contract loomed large in his thoughts, with all the good it might bring to his bakery. But as he gazed out the window at the star-studded sky, another image pushed to the forefront of his mind: Sarah Lapp's warm brown eyes and gentle smile.

Tomorrow was the last community singing before Christmas, a cherished tradition in Maple Creek. Jacob found himself looking forward to it more than usual this year.

Would Sarah be there? Would he hear her clear, sweet voice joining in the familiar hymns?

With a shake of his head, Jacob chided himself for such thoughts. He needed to focus on his business, on providing for Samuel. And yet, as he drifted off to sleep, it was Sarah's face that lingered in his mind, bringing a small smile to his lips.

And in his dreams, her voice, bell-like and loving, filled his ears.

Chapter 11

The crisp December air nipped at Sarah's cheeks as she hurried down the streets of Maple Creek, Emma's small hand clasped tightly in hers. The sun had already begun its descent despite the hour, as they approached that darkest evening of the year.

The sinking orb painted the sky in brilliant shades of orange and pink, peaches and cream as it glinted off the newly fallen snow, like sherbet ice cream. The joyful sound of voices raised in song drifted towards them, growing louder as they approached the town square.

"Hurry, *Mamm*!" Emma tugged at her hand, eyes shining with excitement. "I don't want to miss anything!"

Sarah laughed softly, quickening her pace. "We're almost there, *Liebling*. Look, you can see the lanterns already."

As they rounded the corner, the sight before them took Sarah's breath away. The town square was aglow with the warm light of dozens of lanterns, their gentle flames flickering in the early evening breeze. Familiar faces filled the square, all bundled up against the cold, their breaths visible in small puffs of white as they sang.

Sarah's eyes scanned the crowd, her heart skipping a beat when she spotted Jacob and Samuel near one side. As if he felt her gaze immediately, Jacob looked up, their eyes meeting across the square. He smiled warmly, raising a hand in greeting.

"There's Samuel!" Emma exclaimed, already pulling Sarah towards her friend and his father.

As they approached, Sarah's stomach fluttered a little. Nervousness? Worry? Fear?

Or was it excitement and anticipation?

She and Jacob had been spending more time together since he fixed the oven, but this felt different somehow. More personal, almost, despite the crowds surrounding them.

"Sarah, Emma," Jacob said softly as they joined him and Samuel. "I'm glad you could make it."

"*Hallo*," Sarah replied, hoping the dimming light hid the blush she knew was creeping up her cheeks. Or, that it would be mistaken as a consequence of the cold. "We wouldn't miss it for the world."

As the singing began in earnest, Sarah was swept up in the beauty of the moment. The familiar hymns, sung in harmony with her friends and family and neighbors, filled her with peace and belonging.

The only thing missing was her parents, but they were again traveling for her *mamm's* doctor appointments. The last one was promising, and she was hopeful they would return home before Christmas.

For now, she sang along, her clear soprano blending seamlessly with the voices around her. Beside her, Jacob's rich baritone sent a shiver down her spine that had nothing to do with the cold.

As they moved through "Silent Night," Sarah chanced a glance at him. The soft glow of the lanterns cast a warm

light on his strong features, and she was struck by the
contentment in his expression.

Midway through the song, Jacob's hand brushed against
hers. Sarah's breath caught in her throat, but she didn't
pull away. Instead, she allowed their fingers to brush again,
one more time.

She couldn't feel the warmth of his touch through their
gloves, but her memory filled in the gaps. What would it
feel like to intertwine her fingers with his?

As the final notes of the carol faded away, Sarah was
acutely aware of Jacob brushing her hand with his one
more time. Was that on purpose? She looked up at him,
her heart racing as their eyes met.

"Sarah," Jacob began, his voice low and intense, "I-"

"*Mamm!*" Emma's excited voice cut through the moment. "Can Samuel and I go get some hot chocolate?
Please?"

Sarah blinked, suddenly aware of their surroundings
again. She reluctantly took a half-step back from Jacob,
turning to address her daughter. "Of course, *Liebling*. But
stay where we can see you, *jah*?"

The children scampered off, leaving an awkward silence
between Sarah and Jacob. Sarah busied herself adjusting
her shawl, unsure of what to say.

"It's a beautiful night," Jacob said finally, his gaze fixed
on the starry sky above.

Sarah nodded, grateful for the break in tension. "*Jah*, it
is. *Gott* has blessed us with such a lovely evening for the
winter singing."

They stood in companionable silence for a few moments, watching as Emma and Samuel chatted animatedly
over their steaming cups of hot chocolate.

"They've become fast *freinds*," Jacob observed, a smile in
his voice.

Sarah couldn't help but smile as well. "*Jah*, they have. It's *gut* to see Emma so happy here."

Jacob turned to face her fully, his expression serious. "And what about you, Sarah? Are you happy here?"

The question caught her off guard. Sarah paused, considering her answer carefully. "I am," she said finally. "It hasn't been easy, but... being back in Maple Creek, reopening the bakery... it feels right."

Jacob's eyes softened. "I'm glad," he said softly. "Your return has brought... joy to many in the community."

Sarah's heart fluttered at the implied meaning behind his words. Before she could respond, Emma and Samuel returned, their cheeks rosy from the cold and excitement.

As the evening progressed, Sarah was drawn into conversations with various community members. Mrs. Yoder gushed about Sarah's apple strudel, declaring it "just like your *mamm* used to make!"

Mr. Stoltzfus inquired about special orders for Christmas, his eyes lighting up at the mention of Sarah's famous Lebkuchen. He ordered a dozen on the spot.

Throughout it all, Sarah was acutely aware of Jacob's presence nearby. She caught him watching her more than once, his gaze warm and appreciative. Each time their eyes met, Sarah felt a spark of connection that left her breathless.

As the event drew to a close, Sarah was reluctant to leave, despite the chill seeping into her bones. The evening woke something in her – a sense of belonging, of possibility. While they were preparing to head home, Jacob approached, his expression guarded.

"May we walk you and Emma home?" he asked, his voice low.

Sarah nodded, her heart racing. "That would be lovely, thank you."

The streets of Maple Creek were quiet as they made their way back to King's Sweet Blessings, Emma and Samuel chattering away a few steps ahead of their parents.

"Sarah," Jacob said as they neared the bakery, "I've been meaning to ask you something."

Sarah tensed slightly, unsure of what to expect. "Oh?"

Jacob nodded, his expression earnest. "I was wondering if... well, if you and Emma would like to join Samuel and me for supper sometime this week? Just a simple meal at our home. I know the *kinner* would enjoy spending more time together and I-I would, too."

Sarah's eyes widened in surprise, a warm feeling spreading through her chest. "Oh, Jacob, that would be lovely. We'd be honored."

They had reached the bakery now, but Sarah hesitated on the doorstep, unwilling to end the evening. "Thank you for walking us home," she said softly.

Jacob smiled, the warmth in his eyes making Sarah's heart skip a beat. "It was my pleasure. *Gut* night, Sarah. *Gut* night, Emma."

"Bye!" Samuel said, waving brightly.

Jacob and Samuel headed home, and Sarah stood on the bakery steps, watching them go. Her heart was full of an emotion she hadn't felt in years – hope.

Hope for her bakery, hope for Emma's future, and perhaps hope for something more with Jacob Zook.

Inside, as she tucked Emma into bed, Sarah replayed the evening's events over and over.

"*Mamm*?" Emma's sleepy voice broke through her thoughts. "Are you and Mr. Zook *freinds* now?"

Sarah paused, considering her answer carefully. "*Jah, Liebling*. I think we are."

Emma smiled, her eyes drifting closed. "*Gut*. I like them. Samuel says his *Daed* smiles more when you're around."

Sarah's breath caught in her throat at Emma's innocent observation. She leaned down, pressing a soft kiss to her daughter's forehead. "Sleep well, *mein Schatz*. I love you."

As she prepared for bed, Sarah's eyes fell on the stack of papers on her desk – her bid for the vendor contract. A twinge of guilt passed through her as she thought of Jacob.

Should she tell him about her plans? Did he already know about the opportunity?

But no, this was business. She needed to do what was best for her bakery, for Emma's future.

And yet, as she climbed into bed, Sarah's mind replayed the memory of Jacob's hand brushing hers over and over again, a loop on repeat.

The warmth of his smile, the tenderness in his gaze. For the first time since losing Matthew, she welcomed something she'd thought long extinguished – the possibility of love.

With a sigh, Sarah closed her eyes, letting the events of the day wash over her one last time. The Lebkuchen for her bid, the singing, Jacob's intense gaze... it all swirled together as she drifted off to sleep. Sarah sent up a silent prayer, asking for guidance and praying Gott would help her keep King's Sweet Blessings open for now and for years to come.

And for now, Sarah allowed herself to dream - of success for her bakery, of a bright future for Emma, and just maybe, of a pair of kind blue eyes that saw right into her soul.

Across town, Jacob lay awake in his own bed. The vendor contract weighed heavily on his mind. But now, thoughts of business were intertwined with images of Sarah – her radiant smile, the imagined softness of her hand in his, the way her voice lifted in song.

He thought of the invitation he'd extended for dinner. Was it too forward? Too soon? And yet, the thought of spending more time with Sarah and Emma filled him with a quiet joy he hadn't experienced in years.

As sleep finally began to claim him, Jacob's last conscious thought was a prayer of gratitude. For his son, for his bakery, and for the unexpected gift of Sarah Lapp's return to Maple Creek.

Chapter 12

The next morning dawned bright and clear, a fresh layer of snow blanketing Maple Creek in pristine white. As Sarah opened the bakery, her mind was focused on the day ahead.

She had so much to do. Orders to fill, and preparations to make for her bid that was due for submission tomorrow. With a deep breath, she pushed thoughts of Jacob aside. Today was about business.

The bell above the door chimed, and Sarah looked up to see Mrs. Yoder bustling in, her arms laden with baskets and a warm gray scarf wrapped around her neck.

"*Guder mariye*, Sarah!" she called cheerfully. "Here are those eggs you ordered, plus a few extra, no charge. I thought you might need them, what with all the extra Christmas baking you must have."

Sarah smiled warmly, moving to help Mrs. Yoder with her load. "*Danki*, that's very thoughtful of you."

While she arranged the eggs, Sarah's mind drifted back to the previous evening. The warmth of the community gathering, the joy of singing together, the tender moments with Jacob...

She shook her head slightly, forcing herself to focus on the task at hand. Business. That's where her focus needed to stay.

"You know," Mrs. Yoder said, her voice lowered conspiratorially, "I saw you and Jacob Zook last night at the singing. You two seemed quite... friendly."

Sarah's cheeks heated. "We're neighbors, Mrs. Yoder. And *freinds*."

Mrs. Yoder's eyes twinkled knowingly. "Just *freinds*? *Ach*, if you say so, dear. But I remember when you two were *kinner*, always together. It might be nice to see that again, *jah*?"

Before Sarah could respond, the bell chimed again. She looked up, her heart skipping a beat as Jacob walked in with Samuel in tow.

"*Guder mariye*," Jacob said, his voice warm. "I hope we're not interrupting?"

Sarah shook her head, acutely aware of Mrs. Yoder's curious gaze. "Not at all. What can I do for you two today?"

Jacob chuckled. "Well, this one," he clapped Samuel on the shoulder, "has decided to try out the competition."

He gave her a friendly smile to show no hard feelings as his son pointed out a few items he wanted to try. There was a theme, apparently, with apple danish, apple pie, *and* apple strudel all joining a few Lebkuchen in the bag. Sarah smiled down at the excited boy but felt more than saw Jacob's soft gaze on her.

She glanced at the handsome man and found a smile playing at the corners of his mouth. She busied herself with gathering Samuel's items, trying to ignore the flutter in her stomach.

"Oh, and Sarah?" Jacob said as she handed him his package. "About dinner... would tomorrow evening work for you and Emma?"

Sarah nodded, a smile spreading across her face despite her best efforts to remain composed. Tomorrow, should all go well, she'd win the contract and then spend a lovely evening with Jacob and Samuel.

Sarah couldn't wait.

"*Jah*, that would be *wunderbar*. What can we bring?"

"Just yourselves," Jacob replied, his eyes warm. "We'll take care of the rest."

Jacob and Samuel left, and Sarah watched until they disappeared into Zook's Bakery across the street. She turned to find Mrs. Yoder watching her with a knowing smile.

"Nothing more than *freinds*, eh?" the older woman teased gently.

Sarah shook her head but couldn't keep the smile from her face. "It's just dinner, Mrs. Yoder. For the *kinner*. I want to support Emma's friendship with Samuel."

Mrs. Yoder chuckled, looking wholly unconvinced as she left.

But as she went about her day, preparing batches of cookies and kneading dough for bread, Sarah's thoughts kept drifting to Jacob when she ought to focus on her business. She shook her head and redoubled her efforts to prepare the best Lebkuchen she could for the contract bid. It was almost time.

Across town at the Zook *haus*, Jacob threw himself into his work with renewed vigor after he and Samuel finished supper. The gingerbread village for his bid was coming along nicely, each delicate piece demonstrating his skills.

But as he worked, his mind kept wandering to Sarah. The way her eyes lit up when she smiled, the gentle strength in her voice as she sang, the warmth of her hand in his...

And her apple strudel truly was a work of art. He'd taken a bite from Samuel's pastry when the boy offered, radiating delight after his first taste of the treat.

Perfectly spiced, the right balance of sugar while still letting the apple's flavor dominate the filling. And the pastry itself! Perfectly flaky layers of pure deliciousness.

Jacob shook his head, trying to focus. The vendor contract was too important to let himself get distracted. And yet, as he put the finishing touches on a gingerbread *Englisch* church complete with colorful candies to represent stained glass windows, Jacob wondered what Sarah would think of his creation.

Would she be impressed? Would she offer suggestions, her keen baker's eye-catching details he might have missed?

He sighed. Tomorrow, the bid was due, but he wasn't confident in the design anymore...

Maybe it was time for a break. He left the gingerbread village on the table and went to clean up the dishes in the sink.

A little while later, as he turned back to the village, Jacob's eyes fell on the contract bid paperwork sitting on the counter.

Jacob turned his attention back to the gingerbread village, his gaze lingering on the intricate details he'd so painstakingly crafted in this final version. The tiny gingerbread people with their delicate icing features suddenly looked horribly out of place.

They were beautiful, yes, but were they truly representative of the values he held dear? The miniature Santa Claus, with his bright red clothes on the roof of one house, was especially troublesome.

With a deep breath, Jacob made a decision. He carefully removed the gingerbread figures, Santa Claus first, and set them aside. Then, he began to simplify some of the more elaborate decorations on the houses and buildings.

Englischers might decorate their homes with strings of light, put enormous snowmen on their front lawns, and reindeer on their roofs, but he wasn't *Englisch*. As Jacob worked to adjust the village, a weight lifted from his shoulders.

He didn't want to compromise himself just to win the contract. This felt right, more in line with who he was and what he believed.

"*Gott*," Jacob whispered, his hands steady as he made the adjustments, "guide me in this. Help me to be a *gut* example for Samuel and a *gut* member of this community."

As the clock struck seven, Jacob stepped back to survey his work. The gingerbread village was still impressive, but now it radiated a quiet beauty, a simplicity that spoke of craftsmanship and tradition rather than flashy showmanship. It felt more... honest.

Jacob's mind drifted to Sarah once more. He imagined her working late in her own bakery, pouring her heart into her work just as he did.

The thought no longer filled him with competitive anxiety. Instead, he felt a surge of respect and admiration for her dedication.

And he'd definitely have to pick up her apple strudel again. He could see why everyone raved about it so.

"Samuel?" Jacob called. "*Kumm* here for a moment, please."

His son appeared, looking curious. "*Jah, Daed?*"

Jacob gestured to the modified gingerbread village. "What do you think?"

Samuel studied the display, his eyes widening. "You changed it! It's... different. But I like it. It feels more like us. Simpler."

Jacob felt a rush of pride and relief. "That's exactly what I was going for. Samuel, I've been thinking about what you said, the other day. About Mrs. Lapp and Emma and being *freinds.*"

Samuel looked up at him expectantly.

"You were right," Jacob continued. "Being competitive doesn't mean we can't be kind. In fact, I think it's important that we support each other in this community. Even if we're running different businesses."

A smile spread across Samuel's face. "Does this mean you and Mrs. Lapp are staying *freinds*?"

Jacob chuckled, ruffling his son's hair. "I hope so. We're having them for supper tomorrow, after all. And I promise to try and be more open-minded. You keep being *freinds* with Emma, *jah*? Don't let anyone tell you differently."

Samuel beamed. "I will, *Daed*!"

As Samuel headed back upstairs, Jacob turned to face the window. Tomorrow, if he won the vendor bid from Mr. Anderson and then went home to enjoy supper with Sameul, Emma, and Sarah?

Well.

He couldn't imagine a more perfect day.

The hours stretched on, both Sarah and Jacob immersed themselves in their work, unaware that across town, the other was thinking of them, though both were excited for supper the next day.

And as the full moon rose, casting long shadows across the snow-covered streets of Maple Creek, both bakers continued preparing their entries for the bid, equally unaware of the stiff competition hard at work.

Chapter 13

S arah's hands shook a little as she smoothed down her plain black skirt, her heart racing beneath her neatly pressed dress. The *Englisch* vendor's office loomed before her, its sleek modern exterior a harsh contrast to the simpler buildings of Maple Creek.

She took a deep breath, clutching her carefully prepared bid to her like a shield. A folder with figures and descriptions, plus a basket with samples.

"*Mein Gott,*" she whispered, "please guide me. Let this be Your will."

With one last steadying breath, Sarah pushed open the heavy glass door. The cool air inside washed over her, carrying the unfamiliar scents of chemicals and cologne. She blinked, momentarily disoriented by the bright fluorescent lights and bustling activity.

"May I help you?" a crisp voice asked.

Sarah turned to see a young woman with perfectly coiffed hair and immaculate makeup seated behind a large desk. She looked at Sarah, disinterested but polite.

The baker swallowed hard, suddenly aware of how out of place she must look.

"*Jah*, I mean, yes," Sarah stammered. "I'm here to see Mr. Anderson about the Christmas dessert contract."

The receptionist's eyes widened slightly, but she quickly composed herself. "Ah, of course. Please have a seat. Mr. Anderson will be with you shortly."

Sarah nodded gratefully and made her way to a plush leather chair. As she sat, smoothing her skirts, a familiar voice made her freeze.

"Sarah?"

She looked up, her heart skipping a beat as her eyes met Jacob Zook's startled gaze. He stood in the doorway, a large box in his arms, looking as surprised as she felt.

"Jacob?" Sarah croaked, her voice barely above a whisper. "Wh-what are you doing here?"

Before he could answer, a door opened, and a tall man in a tailored suit emerged. Mr. Anderson.

"Ah, Jacob! You're right on time. And Mrs. Lapp, welcome, welcome, both of you. Please, come in." He smiled at them both, genuinely glad to see them, and gestured for them to follow him.

Sarah rose on shaky legs, following Jacob and Mr. Anderson into the office. Her mind raced.

Jacob was here for the contract too? How could she have been so silly? Of *course* he would bid.

He had a thriving bakery, after all. What chance did she stand against him?

Mr. Anderson called him Jacob, so... the *Englischer* was probably familiar with Zook's Bakery already.

Mr. Anderson settled behind his desk, gesturing for them to sit. "I must say, I'm quite pleased to see you both here. I'm not surprised you know each other, though. Your bakeries are so close together, after all!"

"*Jah*, we're... neighbors, you might say" Jacob said, his deep voice tinged with some emotion Sarah couldn't identify. She was too frazzled to pay much attention to anything right now. "I didn't realize Sarah was bidding as well," he said, voice and face unreadable.

Sarah's cheeks flushed pink though she felt sick. "I-I didn't realize you were, either, Jacob," she admitted softly.

Mr. Anderson's eyebrows rose. "Well, this is unexpected. But we're all here now. I look forward to your proposals. Shall we proceed with the presentations?"

Sarah nodded, her throat suddenly dry. She'd prepared so carefully, practicing her pitch over and over. But now, with Jacob sitting beside her, all her carefully chosen words seemed to evaporate.

"Mrs. Lapp, why don't you go first?" Mr. Anderson suggested.

Sarah took a deep breath, forcing herself to focus. She could do this. She had to, for Emma's sake.

"Mr. Anderson," she began, her voice steadier than she felt. "I'm here to offer you a taste of true Amish tradition for your Christmas party. First, here is a sample for you." She fumbled with the basket, before fishing out the platter with a dozen Lebkuchen for him.

Then, as he dubiously reached out to take one, she opened her bid folder, revealing recipes and carefully written descriptions of her Lebkuchen and other traditional desserts. While she spoke about the recipes passed down through generations, the quality of her ingredients, and her commitment to authenticity, Sarah relaxed.

This was what she knew, what she loved. Her passion shone through, warming her voice, and brightening her eyes. Mr. Anderson took one bite, chewing thoughtfully. He took another bite, and another, finishing the dessert. That was a *gut* sign, wasn't it? He looked pleased with the Lebkuchen.

She could talk about baking and recipes and traditions all day if given the chance. She kept talking, words tumbling faster from her lips.

But as she finished her presentation, Sarah saw the pleased expression after finishing the Lebkuchen had cooled into a polite but somewhat tepid expression on Mr. Anderson's face. Her heart sank.

Had she misjudged? Was her offering too simple, too plain for what he wanted?

"Thank you, Mrs. Lapp," Mr. Anderson said, his tone cordial but noncommittal. "The cookie is quite good and that was very... informative. Jacob, you're up."

Sarah sank back in her chair, watching as Jacob stood. He moved with a quiet confidence that made her stomach churn with anxiety. What could he possibly have that would outshine her family's treasured recipes?

Jacob cleared his throat, his deep voice filling the room. "Mr. Anderson, I'm here to offer you not just desserts, but an experience."

He opened the box he'd brought, and Sarah's breath caught in her throat. Inside was a stunning gingerbread village, complete with tiny, intricately decorated houses, a church with a delicate spire and candied windows.

Even miniature streetlamps and mailboxes crafted from what looked like fondant. It was a work of art far beyond anything Sarah could have imagined.

Now, she second-guessed herself. Would a sugar sculpture display have been a better choice? Those weren't for eating, unlike Lebkuchen.

But maybe the Englisch cared more about how the dessert looked than how it tasted...

As Jacob spoke about his vision for an interactive dessert display, where guests could admire the village and then enjoy pieces of gingerbread stacked strategically around it, Sarah's hopes crumbled. How could her simple Lebkuchen compete with this spectacle?

Mr. Anderson leaned forward, clearly impressed. "This is remarkable, Mr. Zook. The visual appeal is undeniable."

Jacob nodded, but Sarah caught a flicker of something in his eyes. Guilt? Regret?

She wasn't sure, and right now, she hardly cared.

"Well," Mr. Anderson said, leaning back in his chair, "I must say, this decision is easier than I anticipated. While both offerings have their merits, I believe Jacob's proposal aligns more closely with what we're looking for. The visual impact of the gingerbread village will be a talking point for our guests and will make wonderful content for our social media presence."

Sarah sat, heart heavy as a stone. Her breath was labored, as if all of the air was sucked from the room.

She'd lost.

The contract that could have, *would* have, saved her bakery, secured Emma's future... gone.

"Mrs. Lapp," Mr. Anderson continued, his voice softening slightly, "your Lebkuchen are delicious, truly. But for this event, we need something with more... flair."

Sarah nodded numbly, unable to find her voice. She was vaguely aware of Mr. Anderson and Jacob discussing logistics, but their words washed over her like a distant tide.

All she could think about was the stack of bills waiting at home, the temperamental oven that, while repaired, surely needed replacing...

Emma's hopeful face when she'd talked about the contract with her *mamm*.

With Sarah, who had failed.

"Sarah?" Jacob's voice cut through her haze. "Are you all right?"

She blinked, realizing they were both looking at her with concern. "*Ach*, I'm fine," she said, her voice a little shaky. She smiled but feared it was closer to a grimace. Sarah cleared her throat and said, "Congratulations, Jacob. Your village is beautiful."

Without waiting for a response, Sarah stood in one sharp, abrupt motion, gathering her things. "*Danki* for your time, Mr. Anderson," she said, proud that her voice didn't waver. "I-I will leave the rest of the Lebkuchen for you or your employees. I should be going."

She hurried from the office, ignoring Jacob calling her name. Her throat was tight, almost closing up but no matter how many times she swallowed, the lump would not be displaced.

The bright sunlight and clear blue skies above mocked her dark mood. As Sarah climbed into her buggy, she finally allowed the first tears to fall and a shuddering gasp as she fumbled with the reins.

The clip-clop of her horse's hooves on the country road back to Maple Creek usually soothed her, but today it felt like a funeral march.

What would she tell Emma? How could she face her parents, knowing she'd failed to secure the bakery's future?

Lost in her thoughts, Sarah barely noticed the *Englisch* car approaching until it was almost upon her. Suddenly, a loud backfire echoed through the air. Her horse reared, startled by the noise.

"Whoa!" Sarah cried, gripping the reins tightly. For a heart-stopping moment, she thought the buggy might tip. But then her faithful horse settled, snorting nervously but once again under control, nostrils flaring but still.

As the adrenaline faded, leaving her shaky and drained, Sarah let out a bitter laugh.

The failed contract felt like a metaphor for her life. Everything was spiraling out of control, and she was barely hanging on.

With a heavy heart, Sarah sat defeated, head in her hands as she cried. She ought to urge her horse onward, but she dreaded the moment she'd have to face her family and admit her failure.

But even as the tears fell, a small, stubborn spark of determination flickered to life within her. She might have lost this battle, but she wasn't ready to give up on King's Sweet Blessings just yet.

Still, she needed time before she got back up on her feet to fight again. Needed to purge the feelings of failure and helplessness from her heart.

Soon, she'd wipe away her tears and put on a brave face again.

But not yet. Not quite yet.

She needed a little more time, just a little space, all for herself. So, she sat there, crying alone in her buggy.

Chapter 14

J acob's hands clenched and unclenched at his sides as he watched Sarah's buggy disappear down the country road from behind the glass of the *Englisch* office. The taste of victory, so sweet just moments ago, fast turned bitter in his mouth. The image of Sarah's devastated face haunted him, her usually warm brown eyes dulled with disappointment and worry, fear, and defeat.

"Jacob?" Mr. Anderson's voice pulled him back to the present. "Shall we go over the final details?"

Jacob nodded, forcing himself to focus on the task at hand. But as they discussed delivery schedules and payment terms, his mind kept drifting back to Sarah.

He'd known, of course, that winning the contract meant someone else would have to lose. But he'd never imagined it would be her.

"Is everything quite all right, Jacob?" Mr. Anderson asked, peering at him over his glasses. "You seem distracted."

Jacob cleared his throat, embarrassed to be caught wool-gathering. "My apologies," he said. "It's just... Sarah,

I mean, Mrs. Lapp. She's become a friend, lately and I-I hadn't realized we were competing for the same contract."

Mr. Anderson's eyebrows rose. "I see. Well, business is business, Jacob, my good fellow. You can't let personal feelings interfere with professional matters."

Jacob nodded, but the words rang hollow. In the Amish community, personal and professional were often deeply intertwined. How could he celebrate his success, knowing it came at the expense of a widow and her young daughter?

As they wrapped up their meeting, Jacob was itching to leave. He needed to clear his head, to pray for guidance.

The contract would be a boon for his bakery, allowing him to upgrade equipment and perhaps even hire more help. But at what cost?

Finally free of the stuffy office, Jacob climbed into his buggy. The familiar rhythm of his horse's hooves usually brought him peace, but today it felt like an accusation. With each sharp impact of horseshoes on asphalt, he could almost hear Sarah's voice. The rhythm was harsh, betrayed: "How could you? How could you?"

Jacob sighed, running a hand over his beard. He'd done nothing wrong, he reminded himself.

He'd simply presented his best work as any business-man would. And yet... the memory of Sarah's trembling hands as she gathered her things, the slight catch in her voice as she congratulated him... it weighed heavily on his conscience.

Approaching the outskirts of Maple Creek, Jacob's eye was caught by a flicker of movement. A buggy was pulled over on the side of the road, its driver hunched over the reins. With a start, he realized it was Sarah.

Without thinking, Jacob pulled his own buggy to a stop. "Sarah?" he called out, concern coloring his voice. "Is everything all right?"

She looked up, and even from a distance, Jacob saw the tears glistening on her cheeks in the bright sunlight. His heart clenched painfully in his chest.

"I'm fine," Sarah said, her voice barely audible over the rustling of branches in the wind. "Please, just go."

But Jacob couldn't leave her like this. Especially not when he was part of the reason she was in such a state. He climbed down from his buggy, approaching Sarah's carefully.

"What happened? Is it the buggy? The horse?"

Sarah shook her head, wiping hastily at her eyes. "*Nee*, it's not the buggy. Or the horse. She's fine. It's... everything. That contract... it was my last hope, Jacob. Without it, I don't know how I'll keep the bakery open."

The raw pain in her voice hit Jacob like a physical blow. He'd known things were tight for her, but he'd had no idea just how desperate her situation was.

He felt a little sick, recalling when he first heard Sarah, newly returned to town, was reopening her parents' bakery. He'd been upset because it meant he'd no longer have a chance at purchasing their storefront to expand his own business.

Now... would he get that chance? When he no longer even wanted it?

"Sarah, I..." he began, but the words caught in his throat. What could he possibly say to make this right?

She looked up at him then, scrubbing the tears from her face, with her eyes red-rimmed but filled with a quiet dignity that took his breath away.

She sounded tired when she spoke, her voice only shaking a little. "You don't have to say anything, Jacob. You won fair and square. Your gingerbread village... it was beautiful. I just... I need a moment to gather myself before I go tell Emma, that's all."

Jacob's throat closed as pain stabbed behind his sternum. He rubbed the knuckles of one hand against his chest, but it was a pain in the heart, not of the body.

Two roads diverged before him, two different futures he sorely wanted to make converge.

He stood at a crossroads, frozen. On one side was his bakery, his livelihood, the future he'd worked so hard to build for Samuel. On the other was Sarah, this strong, determined woman who'd captured his attention and, if he was honest with himself, his heart.

Frankly, she'd captured his heart when they were *kinner*, only to break it when she left to marry Matthew Lapp. His dear Abigail healed him, only to break it anew when he lost her.

And now? Sarah captured it once more, easy as breathing.

In an instant, Jacob made a reckless decision that might just salvage the disaster of his own making.

"Sarah," he said, his voice low and urgent, "what... what if we worked together on the contract?"

She blinked, confusion replacing the sorrow in her eyes. "What do you mean?"

"I mean," Jacob continued, the idea taking shape as he spoke, "what if we combined our strengths? My gingerbread village with your traditional Lebkuchen and other desserts. Maybe even the sugar sculptures, since the *Englischers* like pretty things. We could create something truly special, something that honors both our skills and our heritage."

Sarah stared at him, hope warring with disbelief on her face. "But... why would you do that? You won the contract outright. Don't you... I *know* you can use the money," she protested. "You're running a business!"

Jacob stepped closer, his heart racing. "Because it's the right thing to do. Because our community is stronger when we work together. And because..." he paused, gathering his courage, "because I care about you, Sarah. More than I realized until today. Until just now."

A soft gasp escaped Sarah's lips, her eyes widening. For a long moment, neither spoke, Jacob's last words hanging in the air between them.

His heart fluttered in his chest. Would she reject the offer? Reject *him*?

Finally, Sarah broke the silence. Her voice was shaking, but this time it wasn't from tears but rather from shock. "Jacob, I... I don't know what to say. This is so unexpected."

"You don't have to say anything right now," Jacob assured her. "About any of it. Just... think about things? We could go back together and present a united front. I know that together we can create something amazing." He gave her a lopsided smile "And I bet if you brought back a sample of those apple strudels, he'd fall all over himself to let you work on the order." A beat later, he chuckled softly.

Sarah looked at him curiously. "What's so funny?"

Jacob shook his head, a wry smile on his face. "I was just thinking... you know, after you left? Mr. Anderson himself said your Lebkuchen tasted better than anything I brought. And I've heard others in the community say the same. Maybe this partnership is meant to be."

Sarah's eyes widened in surprise. "He said that? But then why...?"

"Because my gingerbread village was flashier, I suppose," Jacob admitted. "But flash isn't everything, Sarah. Your b aking... it had history, tradition. It has *heart*. That's something special."

A faint blush colored Sarah's cheeks, and Jacob felt his own face grow warm. He cleared his throat, suddenly

THE WIDOW'S CHRISTMAS COURAGE

aware of how close he was to her, despite the fact she was still in her buggy.

"Well," he said, stepping back slightly, "I-I'm glad nothing's wrong with your buggy. You should go first, and I'll follow to make sure you get back to Maple Creek without any trouble now."

Sarah nodded slowly, a small smile tugging at the corners of her mouth. "I... I'll think about what you said. A-all of it," she added, a little shy. Sarah looked at him, clear-eyed and beautiful, despite the faint traces of tears on her lovely features. "*Danki*, Jacob. Truly."

As Jacob climbed back into his own buggy, his heart lighter than it had been in years. Practically soaring.

She hadn't said no off the bat. So he had a chance then, right?

He didn't know what the future held, but he was excited to find out. With a silent prayer of thanks, he went back to his buggy, gesturing for Sarah to go ahead on the road back to Maple Creek.

"I'll stop by the bakery tomorrow," he called back to her. "We can discuss the details of our... partnership if you're amenable."

Sarah hesitated for a moment, then nodded. "*Jah*, I'd like that. *Gut* night, Jacob."

She smiled at him, waving her goodbye before twitching the reins. Her faithful mare took one step, then another, and before he knew it, they were trotting away, into the distance.

As he watched Sarah's buggy pick up speed, Jacob sent up a silent prayer of thanks. He'd come so close to letting his competitive nature overshadow what truly mattered - community, compassion, and perhaps even love.

And while he was optimistic... as he watched Sarah's buggy disappear around a bend in the road, a small doubt niggled at the back of Jacob's mind. Would she really agree to work with him? Or had he just made a fool of himself, offering to share a contract he'd won fair and square?

And... what if she was just trying to let him down gently? He'd bared his heart to Sarah more than he had to anyone since Abigail. Despite the bright winter sun and clear blue skies, Jacob feared a storm cloud was on the horizon, at least in his heart.

What if he'd just made the biggest mistake of his life?

Chapter 15

The next morning, Sarah walked downstairs, entering King's Sweet Blessings from the kitchen. The familiar click echoed in the pre-dawn stillness, sending a shiver down her spine. She'd left the bread and jam out for Emma, who was independent enough to wake, dress, eat breakfast, and head off to school on her own.

"This is it," she whispered to herself, pushing the door open. The fading scents of yeast and sugar enveloped her, stirring memories and nostalgia, happiness, and security.

Jacob would stop by soon and she...

She didn't know how that made her feel. His offer to share the contract was startling, and his other confession?

Well. She hadn't let herself think about that. Think about what he might be offering.

Think about how much she wanted to accept.

For now, her focus was on the business. At least, until her heart decided to stop humoring her and demanded her full attention.

She was going to work with him on the contract for Mr. Anderson, that wasn't really in question. Though, perhaps she ought to have made it clearer the day before?

But she was so rattled by the circumspect words implying he thought of her as far more than a business rival. More than a neighbor.

More than a friend...

As she flipped on the lights, Sarah's eyes fell on the stack of orders piled high on the counter. The *Englisch* vendor's contract loomed large among them, a daunting task for sure. But she wasn't facing it alone. She unlocked the front door, unsure when Jacob would arrive but unwilling to leave him out in the cold if she was already in the back when he got there.

Sarah's mind drifted back yet again to that moment on the side of the road when Jacob found her at her lowest. She'd felt so beaten down, so close to giving up. Not that she ever would.

But then, like an answer to her prayers, he'd offered to share the contract. It seemed too good to be true, and part of her had wanted to refuse out of pride.

But the look in Jacob's eyes, and then his words... it wasn't pity. It was something else entirely.

The bell above the door chimed, startling Sarah from her reverie. Just as well she'd been lost in thought and hadn't made it back into the kitchen.

Her heart raced as she turned to see Jacob standing in the doorway, his arms laden with supplies.

"*Guder mariye*, Sarah," he said, his deep voice sending a twirling flutter through her chest. She ignored it. Her heart would just have to wait a little longer. "I hope I'm not too early?" he asked, giving her a lopsided smile.

Sarah shook her head, forcing a brisk smile instead of allowing a soft one. This was business. "*Nee*, you're right on time. *Kumm* in, please."

As Jacob set his supplies on the counter, Sarah watched the careful way he moved, as if he was trying not to take up too much space in her bakery.

It was a gesture that both touched and saddened her a little. They'd known each other for years, yet here they were, tiptoeing around each other like strangers. Some of that, maybe even most, was her fault.

"So," Jacob said, breaking the awkward silence. "How do you want to divide the work?"

Sarah took a deep breath, pushing aside her nerves. "Well, I thought we could start with the Lebkuchen. It's a traditional recipe, but I have some ideas for making it a little different, just for the *Englisch* contract."

Jacob nodded, a small smile tugging at his lips. "That sounds *gut*. I brought some of my gingerbread dough. I thought we could work on the village together."

They began to work side by side, and Sarah's shoulders twinged with self-consciousness. Jacob's hands moved with such confidence, his movements sure and practiced. She ended up sneaking glances at him, admiring the way his strong forearms kneaded the dough.

"Is everything all right?" Jacob asked, catching her eye.

Sarah felt her cheeks flush. "*Jah*, of course. I was just... watching your technique. I-it looks *gut*."

Jacob's smile widened, and Sarah's heart skipped a beat. *Focus on the business!*

"*Danki*. I could say the same about you. Your Lebkuchen smells *wunderbar*."

As the morning wore on, Sarah settled into the familiar rhythm of baking. The initial awkwardness began to fade, replaced by a comfortable silence punctuated by the occasional question or comment.

The bell above the door chimed again, and Sarah looked up to see Samuel bursting in with Emma close behind, their cheeks rosy from the cold. She looked at the clock, startled.

School was over already? Where had the day gone?

"*Mamm*!" Emma called out, her eyes shining with excitement. "Can we help? Please?"

Sarah exchanged a glance with Jacob, who nodded his approval. "Of course, *Liebling*. Why don't you and Samuel start by decorating some of the smaller gingerbread houses?"

Jacob brought extras for just this occasion. The children were enthusiastic, and certainly improving, but the contract was too important for their still burgeoning skills.

As the children settled in, their chatter filling the bakery, Sarah felt a warmth spread through her chest. This was what she'd always dreamed of - a bustling bakery full of laughter and love.

"They work well together," Jacob observed, his voice low.

Sarah nodded, watching as Emma showed Samuel how to pipe a delicate icing snowflake. "*Jah*, they do. It's *gut* to see them so happy. I-I think we work well together, too."

He hummed in agreement.

A comfortable silence fell between them as they worked, broken only by the occasional outburst of laughter from the children. Sarah glanced again and again at Jacob, noting the way his brow furrowed in concentration as he carefully constructed a miniature gingerbread bridge.

"You know," Jacob said suddenly, his eyes still fixed on his work, "my Abigail used to make the best snickerdoodles. I've never been able to replicate them."

Sarah's heart clenched at the mention of Jacob's late wife. "Oh? What was her secret?"

Jacob looked up, a wistful smile on his face. "She always said it was love. But I think it might have been the extra cinnamon she snuck in when she thought I wasn't looking."

Sarah laughed softly. "That sounds like something my Matthew would have done. He was always trying to sneak extra chocolate chips into the cookies."

Their eyes met, and for a moment, Sarah felt a connection she rarely ever did. There was understanding in Jacob's gaze, a shared grief that didn't need words.

The moment was broken when Emma called out, "*Mamm*! Can you *kumm* look at our houses?"

As Sarah moved to admire the children's work, she felt Jacob's presence close behind her. His hand brushed against hers as they both reached to steady a wobbly gingerbread roof, sending a spark of awareness through her.

"*Ach*, I'm sorry," Jacob said, quickly withdrawing his hand.

Sarah shook her head, trying to ignore the way her skin tingled where he'd touched her. "It's fine. No harm done."

As the day progressed into evening, Sarah got lost in a comfortable rhythm with Jacob. They moved around each other with ease, anticipating each other's needs and working together seamlessly. She found herself laughing more than she had in years, sharing stories and baking tips as they worked.

Before she knew it, the sun was setting, casting a warm glow through the bakery windows. Sarah stepped back, surveying their day's work with a sense of pride. The counters were lined with trays of Lebkuchen, intricate gingerbread houses, a few delicate sugar sculptures, and gossamer trees and bushes, along with a stunning array of traditional Amish desserts.

"We make a *gut* team," Jacob said, coming to stand beside her.

Sarah nodded, a warmth spreading through her chest that had nothing to do with the heat from the temperamental oven. "*Jah*, we do."

Sarah dallied with the clean-up, reluctant for the day to end. She watched as Jacob helped Emma and Samuel pack up their school things, his gentle manner with the children tugging at her heart.

"Same time tomorrow?" Jacob asked as he prepared to leave.

Sarah nodded, suddenly feeling shy. "*Jah*, that would be *gut*. *Danki* again, Jacob. For-for sharing the contract."

He smiled, his eyes warm. "It's my pleasure, Sarah. Honestly, I don't know if I could do it all by myself. Certainly not as *gut* a job."

After the door closed behind Jacob and Samuel, Sarah stood in the suddenly quiet bakery, her heart full. She wasn't ready to examine those emotions, though. Not yet. She looked down at Emma, who was yawning widely.

"*Kumm* on, *Liebling*," she said softly. "Let's go upstairs."

While they walked up to their cozy home above the bakery, images of Jacob filled her thoughts once again. The way his eyes crinkled when he smiled, the gentleness in his touch when their hands brushed, the understanding in his gaze when they spoke of their late spouses.

Sarah tucked Emma into bed that night and sent up a silent prayer of thanks. Whatever tomorrow might bring, she knew she was no longer facing it alone.

Jacob moved deft hands to adjust the final touches to one of the gingerbread houses. The scent of cinnamon and molasses filled the air, fusing with the aroma of fresh bread that was ever-present in Sarah's bakery. He paused, stepping back to admire their handiwork.

The counters were lined with an impressive array of desserts - traditional Lebkuchen, intricately decorated cookies, Sarah's sugar sculptures, delicate and graceful...

And of course, his signature Gingerbread Village. But it wasn't just the baked goods that filled Jacob with a sense of accomplishment. It was the easy companionship he'd found with Sarah over the past few days.

"What do you think?" Sarah's voice broke through his thoughts. She stood beside him, her cheeks flushed from the heat of the ovens, a smudge of flour on her nose that Jacob found utterly endearing.

"It's *Wunderbar*," he said sincerely. "I think we've outdone ourselves."

Sarah beamed, her entire face lighting up with pride. "I can hardly believe we've accomplished so much in just a few days."

Jacob nodded, his gaze drifting to where Emma and Samuel sat huddled together, working on their school's Christmas quilt project. "We really do make a *gut* team," he said softly, meaning far more than just their baking skills.

Sarah followed his gaze, her expression softening. "*Jah*, we do. It's been... nice, having you here."

Jacob embraced the warmth that spread through his chest at her words. He'd been worried at first, unsure if sharing the contract had been the right decision.

And afraid she was only humoring him for the sake of her business since she never again mentioned his almost confession.

But seeing the light return to Sarah's eyes, watching her bakery come alive with activity and laughter... he knew he'd made the right choice. And even if she never saw him as anything other than a neighbor and friend, he didn't regret the choices he'd made.

Not for a second.

"*Daed*!" Samuel called out. "*Kumm* look at what Emma and I made!"

Jacob moved to admire the children's work, Sarah close beside him. As they leaned in to examine the intricate stitching, their hands brushed once again. This time, neither pulled away.

"It's beautiful," Sarah said, her voice slightly breathless. "You two have done an amazing job."

Jacob nodded in agreement, acutely aware of Sarah's presence beside him. "You should be very proud," he added.

As the children chattered excitedly about their project, Jacob's mind wandered. He thought of the past few days, of the easy rhythm he and Sarah had fallen into.

He thought of the way she laughed at his jokes, the thoughtful furrow of her brow as she concentrated on a particularly intricate design. He thought of the quiet moments they'd shared, speaking of their late spouses and the challenges of single parenthood.

"Jacob?" Sarah's voice pulled him back to the present. "Are you okay?"

He blinked, realizing he'd been staring. "*Jah*, sorry. Just lost in thought."

Sarah's expression softened. "*Gut* thoughts, I hope?"

Jacob nodded, feeling a sudden surge of courage. "Very *gut* thoughts," he said softly. "Sarah, I..."

But before he could finish his thought, Emma piped up. "*Mamm*, can we have some hot chocolate? It's so cold outside!"

Sarah laughed; the moment was broken. "Of course, *Liebling*. Why don't you and Samuel go wash up while I prepare it?"

The children scampered off leaving Jacob alone with Sarah once again. The air between them danced with static, charged with unspoken words and growing feelings.

"Sarah," he began again, his heart racing. "I wanted to thank you. Not just for helping with the contract, but for... everything. These past few days have been..."

"Special?" Sarah supplied, her eyes meeting his.

Jacob nodded, feeling a rush of relief at her understanding. "*Jah*, special. I haven't felt this... content in a very long time."

Sarah's cheeks flushed, but she didn't look away. "I feel the same way, Jacob. Having someone to share the work with, to talk to... but mostly, I think it was *wunderbar* because, well, because it was you," she finished, blinking but never breaking eye contact.

Jacob took a deep breath, gathering his courage. "Sarah, I know this might seem sudden. And, of course, there is no... no obligation, no pressure," he said, fumbling with his words. Jacob coughed into one hand, looking away before meeting her eyes again, steady and hopeful.

"Sarah Lapp, would you allow me to court you?" he asked, soft and sincere.

Sarah's eyes widened, and for a heart-stopping moment, Jacob feared he'd overstepped. But then a slow smile spread across her face, lighting up her eyes in a way that took his breath away.

"Jacob Zook," she breathed more than spoke, "I would be honored."

He leaned down, lifting one hand to clasp her smaller fingers between his. She tilted her head up, tongue darting out to wet her lips as her eyes fluttered closed.

He felt her breath on his cheek, moving closer, closer, closer...

Just then, the patter of small feet announced the return of Emma and Samuel. Jacob stepped back, his heart soaring even as he struggled to compose himself.

A flush rose bright and high on Sarah's cheekbones, but she didn't let his hand go, squeezing it and smiling up at him, with a look that said, *of course* and *we're in this together* and *later...*

"Is the hot chocolate ready, *Mamm*?" Emma asked, oblivious to the monumental shift which the *kinner* interrupted. Which was just as well, really.

Jacob wanted to tell Samuel himself, and surely Sarah would want the same for Emma.

Sarah blinked as if coming out of a daze. "Oh! Not yet, *Liebling*. I'll get started on it now."

As Sarah busied herself with preparing the hot chocolate, Jacob caught her eye across the kitchen. The look they shared was full of promise, of hope for a future neither of them had dared to even imagine such a short time ago.

Life would still be filled with challenges, from the completion of the *Englisch* contract to discussions about merging their families and businesses...

But Jacob knew they would face them together. And as he watched Sarah laughing with the children, her eyes sparkling with joy, he sent up a silent prayer of thanks.

Gott's plan, it seemed, was far greater and more beautiful than anything Jacob ever dreamed.

Chapter 16

S arah frowned as she carefully arranged the steaming dishes on the long wooden table, working to fit each dish like a puzzle. The aroma of roast turkey, freshly baked bread, and her famous apple pie filled the air, mingling with the scent of pine from the simple evergreen boughs adorning the mantel.

Only days since Jacob asked to court, and she was almost delirious with happiness. They'd finished the *Englisch* contract and delivered it to Mr. Anderson.

The man was delighted to learn that they had decided to collaborate, and even more delighted after he tried her apple strudel, just as Jacob predicted. He thanked them both profusely, and even added a bonus to the payment.

Now, it was Christmas Day. She paused, taking in the scene before her - her family and Jacob's gathered together in her parents' home, the sound of laughter and cheerful chatter warming her heart even more than the crackling fire in the hearth.

Her *daed* was more relaxed than she'd seen in a long time. Probably because he and her *mamm* were back home, for good this time. Her *mamm's* treatments went well, and while she was still weak, the doctors said she'd make a full recovery.

"Sarah, *Liebling*," her mother called from the kitchen, "Can you bring the cranberry sauce?"

"*Jah, Mamm*," Sarah replied, hurrying to fetch the last dish. As she re-entered the dining room, her eyes met Jacob's across the table. His warm smile sent a flutter through her chest, and she felt her cheeks flush.

"Everything looks *Wunderbar*, Sarah," Jacob's mother praised, her eyes twinkling. "You've outdone yourself."

Sarah ducked her head modestly. "*Danki*, but I had plenty of help. We all contributed."

Everyone took their seats, and Sarah's father cleared his throat. "Shall we bow our heads in prayer?"

A hush fell over the room as they bowed their heads. Sarah felt Jacob's strong, calloused fingers entwined with hers under the table, sending a warmth spreading up her arm.

In silent prayer, each person communed with *Gott*, thanking Him for the bountiful meal, for bringing everyone together, for all of His blessings. Sarah prayed fervently, grateful for His guidance and love, especially during the difficult weeks and months and years past.

And, most of all, for guiding her back to Maple Creek. Back to Jacob.

Back to love.

Soon, the room was filled with the clink and rattle of silverware and dishes underscoring animated conversation. Compliments to the cooks rang up and down the table as well.

"*Mamm*, can Samuel and I exchange our gifts now?" Emma asked, her blue eyes shining with excitement.

Sarah glanced at Jacob, who nodded his approval. "After we finish eating, *Liebling*," she said gently. "Remember, patience is a virtue."

Emma pouted for a moment but quickly brightened when she turned to Samuel, whispering conspiratorially about their handmade presents. The *kinner* were thrilled when their parents sat them down and explained they were now courting, more excited to become siblings than they were to gain another parent each. As the meal progressed, Sarah almost teared up at how naturally their two families seemed to fit together.

Her parents, still beaming with pride over the success of the bakery collaboration, were deep in conversation with Jacob's father about expanding their bakeries and mapping out possible delivery routes. Jacob's mother was fussing over Sarah's *mamm*, insisting she take seconds of everything to help with her recovery.

"You have your color back, Rachel," Mrs. Zook said warmly. "I'm so glad to see you up and about."

Sarah's mother smiled, patting Mrs. Zook's hand. "*Jah*, I'm feeling much better. And having everyone here..." she paused, her eyes misting slightly. "It's the best medicine I could ask for."

As Sarah began clearing the dishes, she felt a gentle touch on her arm. She turned to find her mother beside her, a knowing smile on her face.

"Let me help you, Sarah," she said softly. "We can talk while we work."

In the kitchen, while they washed and rinsed plates, her *mamm* drying, Rachel King broached the subject she'd clearly been waiting to discuss.

"So," she began, her tone casual but her eyes twinkling, "you and Jacob seem to be getting along very well."

Sarah felt her cheeks warm. "*Jah*, we are. He's been so helpful with the bakery, of course, with the oven and the contract and-" She stopped, clearing her throat and staring intently at the dish in front of her. The sauce might be tough to scrape off.

"And?" her mother prompted gently.

Sarah sighed, a small smile tugging at her lips. "And... there's something more there, as you know. But it's all happening so fast, *Mamm*. Is it wrong to feel this way so quickly? We've hardly been back in Maple Creek..."

Her mother set down the dish she was drying and turned to face Sarah fully. "*Liebling*, listen to me. Matthew would want you to be happy. He loved you so much, and he wouldn't want you to be alone forever. *Gott* has a plan for all of us, and if that plan includes Jacob Zook, wel l..." She paused, her eyes twinkling mischievously, before adding, "I'd say you'd be a fool not to embrace it."

Sarah laughed softly, pulling her mother into a tight hug. "*Danki, Mamm*. I needed to hear that."

As they returned to the dining room, Sarah's eyes were drawn to Jacob, who was deep in conversation with her father. The serious expression on both their faces made her wonder what they were discussing.

Emma's excited voice broke through her thoughts. "*Mamm*! Can we exchange gifts *now*? Please?"

Sarah nodded, her heart warming at the sight of Emma and Samuel's eager faces. "*Jah*, go ahead."

The children scampered to retrieve their carefully wrapped packages, presenting them to each other with shy smiles.

"You first," Emma insisted, bouncing on her toes.

Samuel carefully unwrapped his gift, revealing a hand-knitted scarf in shades of blue and gray. His face lit up with delight. "It's perfect! Did you make this yourself, Emma?"

Emma nodded proudly. "*Mamm* helped me learn, but I did most of it myself. Do you really like it?"

"I love it," Samuel assured her, immediately wrapping it around his neck. "Now open yours!"

Emma tore into her package, gasping as she pulled out a small, intricately carved wooden box. The lid was adorned with a simple daisy pattern.

"Samuel," she squealed, "it's beautiful! Did you make this?"

Samuel nodded, his cheeks flushing slightly. "*Daed* helped me with some of the trickier parts, but I did most of it. Look inside!"

Emma carefully opened the box to find a few matching wooden blooms nestled inside. She threw her arms around Samuel, hugging him tightly. "*Danki*! I love it so much! You're gonna be the best big *bruder* ever!"

As the adults watched the children's exchange with fond smiles, Sarah felt a warmth spread through her chest. This was what Christmas was all about - family, love, and the joy of giving.

The families gathered in the living room, and soon the air was filled with the sound of traditional Christmas hymns. Sarah's clear soprano blended beautifully with Jacob's rich baritone, their voices weaving together in perfect harmony.

As the last notes of "Silent Night" faded away, Jacob caught Sarah's eye, nodding towards the front door. She understood his unspoken request and rose to follow him outside.

The crisp winter air nipped at Sarah's cheeks when they stepped onto the porch. The world was blanketed in white, the snow glistening like diamonds under the starry sky. Jacob took her hand, leading her to the old porch swing.

"It's beautiful out here," Sarah murmured, leaning into Jacob's warmth.

"*Jah*, it is," he agreed, his voice low. "But not as beautiful as you."

Heat rushed up her neck and cheeks, and not just from the cold. She turned to face Jacob, her heart racing at the intensity in his eyes.

"Sarah," he began, taking both her hands in his, "these past days have been... *Wunderbar*. Working with you, getting to know you and Emma better... it's made me realize something."

"What's that?" Sarah asked softly, hardly daring to breathe. Jacob's thumbs traced gentle circles on the backs of her hands, making her glad she'd not bothered with gloves.

"That I don't want to wait any longer, Sarah Lapp. That I don't need to. I've already spoken to your *daed*, and he's given his blessing. But what I want to know is this: will you marry me?"

Sarah's heart soared. She'd been hoping for this, dreaming of it even, but to hear the words spoken aloud... it was more than she could have imagined. All her fears about falling too hard, too fast, for this handsome, amazing man vanished into nothing.

Instead, she was filled with steadfast certainty, deep and sure as the roots of an old forest. The future unfurled before her, a sturdy blossom ready to drink up all the love and joy ahead.

"*Ach*, Jacob," she breathed, her eyes shining with unshed tears of joy. "*Jah. Jah*, I would be honored."

Jacob's face broke into a radiant smile, and before Sarah could react, he leaned in and pressed his lips to hers in a soft, warm kiss. She pressed back, wishing the moment would last forever. It was brief and chaste, but it sent sparks shooting through Sarah's entire body.

As they pulled apart, both slightly breathless, Jacob rested his forehead against hers. "*Danki*, Sarah. You've made me the happiest *mann* in Maple Creek. *Nee*, in the whole wide world."

Sarah laughed softly, her heart full to bursting. "And you've made me the happiest woman."

They sat in comfortable silence for a few moments, basking in the glow of new love and endless possibilities, hands clasped. Finally, Jacob looked over his shoulder at the *haus*. He stood, not letting go of her hand.

"We should head back inside before they send out a search party," he said with a chuckle.

Sarah nodded, allowing Jacob to help her up. As they walked hand in hand back towards the warmth and light of the house, she sent up a silent prayer of thanks.

This Christmas brought her more blessings than she could have ever imagined - a thriving bakery, her *mamm's* recovery, and now, the promise of an even bigger, loving family and future with Jacob. As they crossed the threshold, the sounds of laughter and cheerful conversation washed over them.

Emma and Samuel were showing off their gifts to the grandparents, while the adults chatted contentedly over cups of steaming coffee. Sarah's mother caught her eye, a knowing smile spreading across her face as she took in their clasped hands and flushed cheeks.

Sarah blushed even deeper but didn't fight the smile blooming on her face. This was what coming home truly meant. Not just to a place, but to people who loved you, to a community that supported you, and to a future full of hope and promise.

As Jacob squeezed her hand gently, Sarah knew in her heart that the future ahead would only glow bright and taller and bring even more bounty into their lives. And with *Gott's* blessing, their love would only grow stronger with each passing day.

Epilogue

The harsh winter air bit at Sarah's cheeks as she hurried across the street, her arms laden with freshly baked cinnamon rolls. The early morning sun cast a golden glow over the snow-covered streets of Maple Creek, the familiar sounds of horse hooves and the rattle of buggy wheels heralding the start of another day.

As she approached Zook's Sweet Blessings, Sarah smiled at the cheerful Christmas wreath adorning the door, green with springs of bright red holly berries. It was just over a year since she and Jacob officially combined their bakeries, and with each passing day, she was happier than ever that they made that decision.

The bell above the door chimed as Sarah entered, the warm aroma of yeast and sugar enveloping her like a comforting hug. Jacob looked up from arranging a display of Lebkuchen, his face breaking into a wide smile at the sight of her.

"*Guder Mariye, mein Schatz*," he said, crossing the room to relieve her of her burden. "You're here early."

Sarah laughed softly, stretching up on her toes to press a quick kiss to his cheek. "The twins decided that sleep was overrated this morning. I thought I might as well put the time to *gut* use."

That morning, the soft cries woke her after Jacob left for the bakery. Sarah moved towards the sound, her heart swelling with love as she caught sight of their three-month-old twins, Abigail and Matthew, nestled in their bassinet. Little Abigail was fussing, her tiny fists waving in the air.

"Shh, *Liebling*," Sarah had cooed, gently lifting the baby into her arms. "*Mamm's* here."

And now, her *mamm* was there to watch over the *bopplin*, and would bring them with her later in the morning.

How much her life had changed in two short years! From the struggling widow who returned to Maple Creek with nothing but hope and determination, to the contented wife and mother and successful business owner she was now – it was more than she ever dreamed on that first day back in Maple Creek.

But now, it was time to work.

━━━ *ele* ━━━

Two days later, on Christmas morning, Sarah and Jacob sat in their kitchen enjoying a moment of peace and a hot cup of coffee together. After a little while, the sound of excited whispers and giggles drifted down from upstairs, growing louder with each passing moment. Sarah and Jacob exchanged knowing smiles.

"I think the *kinner* are awake," Jacob said, his eyes twinkling. "Shall we see what they're up to?"

Before Sarah could respond, Emma and Samuel tumbled into the kitchen, their cheeks flushed with excitement.

"*Mamm! Daed*!" Emma exclaimed, her blue eyes shining. "Can we open our gifts now? Please?"

Samuel, ever the protective older brother, shushed her gently. "Emma, remember, the *bopplin* are sleeping."

Sarah's heart swelled with pride at the sight of their blended family. Emma, now ten, and Samuel, eleven, had taken to their roles as older siblings with enthusiasm and love. It warmed her heart to see how naturally they had all come together.

"Of course, we can open gifts," Jacob said, his voice warm. "But not yet. First, let's have some breakfast. Your *Mamm* made cinnamon rolls."

"Don't worry," Sarah said wryly. "I made a batch with your *daed's* recipe and one with mine, too."

With the family gathered around the weathered, well-loved kitchen table, Sarah sighed in contentment. The struggles, the doubts, and the moments of fear on her journey to this moment all faded, overshadowed by the joy and love that filled their lives every day.

The family ate breakfast, and then Sarah went to fetch the twins, bringing them downstairs. Samuel and Emma each commandeered a sibling, playing with them with pure delight.

A little later, a knock on the front door was followed by the sound of it opening. Sarah looked to see both sets of grandparents entering, their arms laden with gifts and dishes for their Christmas feast.

"Merry Christmas!" Sarah's mother called out, her eyes lighting up at the sight of the twins. "Oh, let me see my beautiful *grandkinner*!"

"Now you can open gifts," Sarah said. As the grandparents cooed over the babies and Emma and Samuel carefully opened their gifts, Sarah felt Jacob's fingers slip between hers. She squeezed tight, drawing strength and comfort from his presence.

"Happy?" he murmured, his breath warm against her ear.

Sarah nodded, unable to find words to express the depth of her contentment. "More than I ever thought possible," she murmured back.

The morning passed in a blur of laughter, joy, and the warmth of family togetherness. As Sarah moved to start preparing their Christmas feast, Jacob caught her hand.

"Wait," he said, a mischievous glint in his eye. "I have one more gift for you."

, Sarah followed him to their now-shared office. Jacob reached behind the door and pulled out a large, flat package.

"Open it," he urged, his excitement palpable.

Sarah carefully unwrapped the gift, gasping as she revealed a beautiful hand-painted sign. "Zook's Sweet Blessings," it read in elegant script, with intricate designs of flowers and wheat sheaves adorning the borders.

"Oh, Jacob," she breathed, tears pricking at the corners of her eyes. "It's beautiful."

"I thought we could hang it above the front door, under the awning," he said softly.

Sarah nodded, too overwhelmed to speak. She remembered the day they had decided to combine their bakeries, the excitement and trepidation they both felt. Her parents gave their blessing without hesitation, understanding that this was not just a business decision, but yet another symbol of the joining of two families, two legacies.

"And that's not all," Jacob continued, pulling an envelope from his pocket. "Mr. Anderson called the bakery yesterday. He wants to extend our contract for another three years. Said our Christmas desserts are the talk of the town, and he can't imagine his parties without our desserts. Especially your Lebkuchen," he added as the corners of his eyes crinkled.

Sarah's eyes widened. "Three years? *Ach*, Jacob, that's wonderful news!"

As they embraced, celebrating their success, a commotion from the kitchen caught their attention. They rushed back to find Emma standing on a chair, flour covering her from head to toe, while Samuel tried desperately to catch a cascade of sugar pouring from an overturned bag.

"We wanted to help with the Christmas pudding," Emma explained sheepishly.

For a moment, Sarah and Jacob stood in stunned silence. Then, almost in unison, they burst into laughter. Soon, the entire family was laughing, the joy of the moment overshadowing the mess.

"*Ach*, how about you help clean this up, and then we can work on it, together?" Sarah said, wiping tears of mirth from her eyes.

As they all pitched in to clean up, working together with easy familiarity, a wave of gratitude washed over her. This was what Christmas was truly about – not perfect moments, but real ones, filled with love, laughter, and family.

Later that evening, after the last dishes were cleared away and the twins were settled into their cribs, Sarah found herself once again on the front porch of their home. Jacob joined her, wrapping a warm blanket around both their shoulders.

"Remember two Christmases ago?" he asked softly, his arm drawing her close. "When we came out to the porch?"

Sarah nodded, thinking back to that magical night when Jacob proposed. "How could I forget? It was the beginning of all this," she said, gesturing to the bakery, the house, their life together.

"I thank *Gott* every single day for bringing you back to Maple Creek," Jacob murmured, pressing a kiss to her temple. "I love you, Sarah Zook."

Sarah turned to face him, her heart full to bursting. "And I thank Him for giving me the courage to *kumm* back. For leading me back home. For leading me to you."

As they stood there, wrapped in each other's arms, watching the quiet snow gently falling, Sarah closed her eyes, pure peace suffusing her. The future wouldn't be perfect - how could it be, raising four children while running a successful bakery?

But with Jacob's love and their faith in *Gott*, the Zooks could face anything.

The soft cries of the twins drifted from inside, and Sarah smiled. "Duty calls," she said with a laugh.

Jacob nodded, taking her hand as they made their way back inside. "Together?" he asked, his eyes shining with love.

"Always," Sarah replied, her heart full of joy and gratitude for the blessed future that lay ahead. "I love you, Jacob Zook."

He pressed a kiss to her lips, soft and familiar and warm and perfect.

As they entered the *haus*, the sign he'd given her for their bakery glinted in the moonlight streaming through the door, a tangible reminder of the power of faith, love, and the sweet blessings that come when two hearts find their way home.

Thank you so much for reading, I hope you enjoyed the story!

Sign up for my newsletter for new releases, updates, and more.

About Miriam Beiler

Please feel free to visit my Facebook page:
https://www.facebook.com/miriambeilerauthor

Or email me: **miriam@miriambeiler.com**

Made in the USA
Middletown, DE
28 December 2024